lso by Roberta Updegraff
n Large Print:

Puzzle in Patchwork

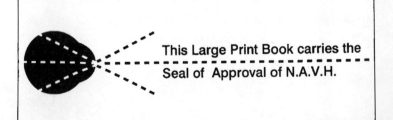

This Large Print Book carries the
Seal of Approval of N.A.V.H.

CU00794047

The
Baffling Beques

Guideposts
Church Choir Mysteries™

The
Baffling Bequest

Roberta Updegraff

Thorndike Press • Waterville, Maine

Copyright © 2003 by Guideposts, Carmel, New York 10512.

Published in 2004 by arrangement with
Guideposts Book Division.

Thorndike Press® Large Print Christian Mystery.

The tree indicium is a trademark of Thorndike Press.

The text of this Large Print edition is unabridged.
Other aspects of the book may vary from the original edition.

Set in 16 pt. Plantin by Al Chase.

Printed in the United States on permanent paper.

Library of Congress Cataloging-in-Publication Data

Updegraff, Roberta.
  The baffling bequest / Roberta Updegraff.
    p. cm. — (church choir mysteries)
  ISBN 0-7862-7094-2 (lg. print : hc : alk. paper)
  1. Inheritance and succession — Fiction.   2. Church
musicians — Fiction.   3. Women detectives — Fiction.
4. Choirs (Music) — Fiction.   5. Sisters — Fiction.
6. Widows — Fiction.   7. Large type books.   I. Title.
II. Series.
PS3621.P38B34 2004
813'.6—dc22   2004042353

Eileen M. Berger,
mentor and dear friend.
You continue to be a shining example
as you share your time and craft
with aspiring writers.

And Elizabeth Kramer Gold
for taking the risk on me.
Your quiet devotion to family
is a model for all.

As the Founder/CEO of NAVH, the only national health agency solely devoted to those who, although not totally blind, have an eye disease which could lead to serious visual impairment, I am pleased to recognize Thorndike Press* as one of the leading publishers in the large print field.

Founded in 1954 in San Francisco to prepare large print textbooks for partially seeing children, NAVH became the pioneer and standard setting agency in the preparation of large type.

Today, those publishers who meet our standards carry the prestigious "Seal of Approval" indicating high quality large print. We are delighted that Thorndike Press is one of the publishers whose titles meet these standards. We are also pleased to recognize the significant contribution Thorndike Press is making in this important and growing field.

Lorraine H. Marchi, L.H.D.
Founder/CEO
NAVH

* Thorndike Press encompasses the following imprints: Thorndike, Wheeler, Walker and Large Print Press.

Acknowledgments

Thanks to all the wonderful support folks in my life. Hugs to my darling husband Mark for running umpteen errands, taking over the taxi service and, most of all, giving me lots of encouragement (the massages were great, too). Kisses to Katie (our youngest and only child still at home) for being a good sport about being forgotten or picked up late. *Abbracci* to our exchange student Dario Recalcati for all the pick-me-ups, cups of coffee and Italian cookies that appeared at my computer just when I needed a break.

Special thanks to Eileen M. Berger, my wonderful mentor and friend, for brainstorming the plot with me. I appreciate all the support you've given me through the years. Hugs to Roberta Brosious for all your help — you are the dearest of friends. Kudos to all the West Branch Christian Writers and St. David's Christian Writer's Association. I appreciate you all!

Accolades to my great editors at Guideposts Books and Inspirational Media Division! Michele Slung does a great job of making my manuscript read better, and Stephanie Castillo Samoy is even sweeter in person. Thanks, ladies, for the wonderful day in New York City. I appreciate you all more than words can convey!

1

"A birthday party for a *dead* person? Now *that* takes the cake!" Estelle Livett smacked the topmost music folder in front of her.

Eternal Hope's outspoken chorister had a knack for arousing ire in even the most affable of her fellows, but this time, Gracie could appreciate her friend's response. The combined home-going and birthday bash in honor of Hazel Rohleder's recently deceased sister *did* seem to take the cake, quite literally.

Gracie recalled her own reaction when she'd heard the idea. However, Gracie had been willing to grant that the idea of celebrating Mabel's going to heaven along with celebrating the sisters' joint birthday made some kind of sense.

"The Rohleder's always have had their own way of doing things," Marybeth Bower offered by way of explanation. The police chief's wife in Willow Bend, Indiana, tended to look on the bright side of things.

Estelle was not to be appeased. "That's

putting it mildly! Hazel's wardrobe looks like early Goodwill. And those ridiculous shoes! How can any self-respecting senior traipse around town in moccasins and knee socks?"

Young Amy Cantrell put her hand up to her mouth to conceal a giggle.

"She's making an absolute fool of herself!" Estelle insisted, glaring at Amy.

"I wasn't laughing at Miss Rohleder," Amy protested, not lowering her gaze under Estelle's stare. "The thing is, she isn't afraid to be herself. What you said struck me as funny, that's all. As if her choice in shoes has something to do with her self-respect."

"*Hmmph.* It's not her fashion sense I object to! She can be as eccentric as she wants — in her own home," Estelle declared. "But dragging us into her flights of fancy is just too much. I'm simply trying to spare our church this embarrassment."

"She's one of our oldest members, and I don't think any sort of birthday party in her honor is too much to ask," Marybeth now said. "Anyway, she and Mabel were twins, so it's fitting we include Mabel — in spirit, that is."

Estelle still glowered. "Humoring her isn't going to solve the problem. And your husband providing taxi service when she gets discombobulated or lost isn't helping either."

Oh, my, Gracie thought. She wished never to think ill of anyone, but Estelle certainly pushed the limits. Nevertheless, Gracie had long ago determined to look for the cream filling in even the crustiest of souls.

She pointed out gently, "We *all* become forgetful with age, Estelle. I've misplaced my car in the mall parking lot on more than one occasion! And how many times have you walked into a room without remembering what you meant to do there? More than once, I'll bet!"

Marybeth chuckled. "You'll have to tie a ribbon to Fannie Mae's antenna, like I do. But don't use red. It's much too popular. I tied a red one to my car, and the kids and I stumbled around for twenty minutes trying to find *our* silver minivan. I think half the county owns the same make!"

"It's not a joking matter," Estelle insisted. "There comes a time when someone has to intervene in cases like this, particularly if the person doesn't have family."

"Herb has had to take Hazel home on several occasions," Marybeth admitted. "But if he didn't think she could take care of herself, he would have brought it to the attention of someone better qualified who could help her."

It had been Herb Bower's diplomacy that had diffused a potential crisis in the first place. That was before Mabel died, and when both sisters were still driving on a regular basis. After Mabel's third fender-bender in as many months, the police chief went to Pastor Paul Meyer and suggested that the Eternal Hope family offer transportation.

Mabel was happy to accept, but Hazel, the more stubborn of the pair, insisted on continuing to get herself where she needed to be on her own. She flat out refused to telephone the person in charge of transporting the congregation's elderly and disabled members for that month. Thankfully, however, Hazel generally preferred walking to driving.

Gracie understood Hazel's desire to hold on to her independence. The two sisters had taken care of each other for most of their lives. "I give Hazel credit for living on her own," she said.

Estelle crossed her arms. "Credit's fine, but it won't keep her from harming herself or someone else." Now her angry expression took in Barb Jennings, their choir director and organist.

Marybeth looked over at Gracie. The expression on her face indicated that she, too, sensed an upcoming confrontation. Barb, who tended to be high-strung, had had more than a few run-ins with the self-appointed choir diva.

Gracie recalled Barb's fondness for the elderly sisters, and hoped to diffuse the tension by saying, "Mabel was once the church organist, wasn't she?"

"Yes, indeed. But only on a very part-time basis in recent years, since I came." Barb glanced at Estelle before turning her attention to Gracie and the others.

"She actually helped me get used to our quirky old pipe organ. I complained that it was too difficult, and wanted to give up, but Mabel would say, 'A smooth sea never made a skillful sailor.' And that's how she handled every problem or adversity, including her illness."

"That's a lovely eulogy," Marybeth commented appreciatively, in an attempt to defuse the tension.

Rick Harding, their African-American tenor, broke in, "Mabel was special, all right. Lillian was privileged to have her for an adopted grandmother."

He paused, obviously dealing with his own sadness at losing a valued member of

13

the Eternal Hope flock. "Mabel prided herself on her eccentricity, and we loved her for it. Lillian felt right at home with a woman who was not afraid to wear Victorian hats to tea parties with little girls, and squeal when she got stuck with the Old Maid."

His grin widened. "And Hazel is no different. Hallelujah for their delightful eccentricities!"

"I know you all were with her earlier on the day she died," Barb recalled. "Hazel told me so later, when I came to visit. There was a darling watercolor your Lillian had painted propped on Mabel's bedside table."

"She was in the mood to settle her accounts when we were there," Rick said. "Mabel'd packed her bags, so to speak, and wanted to say good-bye. She had a list of instructions to the folks she was leaving behind, and wonderful words of encouragement for Lillian. Mabel was so calm that I wondered if the old gal had received confirmation from God that she was going home that very day."

"She wanted to say good-bye," Barb said softly. "There were things on that list she needed to go over with me, as well. She knew I loved that old harpsichord in the den, and she wanted me to have it."

Rick nodded. "She wanted to be sure

Lillian got that purple plumed hat that she wore to their tea parties."

Gracie thanked God for Pastor Paul's idea of matching up the oldest and youngest members of their congregation as prayer partners. Lillian had been Mabel's "spiritual granddaughter." It was wonderful how it was working out so well, bringing the generations together.

As Rick and Barb shared their memories of their final encounters with the dying woman, it was clear that Mabel had been the one comforting them all, assuring them of her certainty about what was to come.

"Mabel told Lillian that she was terribly tired," Rick said. "And Lillian, with a child's wisdom, gave her permission to go to sleep. She wanted her mom to read Mabel a bedtime Bible story, just like we do at home each night."

Taking a deep breath, Rick paused in his recollection for an instant, then continued. "Mabel agreed that sleep *did* feel a little like heaven, because then the pain disappeared. She thanked Lillian for being so wise and, a second later, closed her eyes."

Gracie's best friend Marge Lawrence hugged Rick. "This is for Lillian."

"Hazel's suffering too, you know. As merciful as Mabel's death was, it hasn't been easy for Hazel," Rick reminded them. "She took care of her sister, and watching Mabel's health deteriorate broke her heart. I could see it in her eyes. She's tired now, but who can blame her? If people want to criticize her, saying she's losing touch with reality, they should look at what she's just been through. I admire her myself for keeping her sister at home."

There were nods of agreement all around.

"We all do!" Marge declared.

Gracie reminded them now, "She only wants her sister to have a proper sendoff to heaven. It's their eightieth birthday and they've always celebrated them together."

"Lillian and she used to talk about plans for the party," Rick recalled.

"Hazel wants to honor her sister's wish, that's all," Gracie went on. "She's a little afraid, though, that folks won't come. We'd all admit Mabel was the more easygoing of the two. Hazel can be a bit prickly at times."

She suddenly had an idea. "Maybe we could take it on — give them both a birthday party."

"What a great idea!" Amy said.

Estelle only *tsked*.

Barb hesitated, about to say something. The choir director and the temperamental soprano were often at odds. But Gracie

16

sensed it went deeper this time.

Marybeth now turned to Estelle. "We can do this for Hazel, can't we? She just lost her twin, and they've both been longtime members of this church, after all."

"Not regular attendees," Estelle pointed out.

"They came as often as Mabel's health allowed." Gracie was getting exasperated.

"In their day," Barb began, "most respectable women married young, but instead the Rohleders went off to a women's college back east. They then ran a small art gallery together until the aunt who'd raised them took sick. They came back to take care of her, and they were odd, by most folks' standards, even then."

She went on, "But, to me, they were splendid examples of womanhood. They had their own lives and seemed happy with their choices. While they lived here and took care of their aunt, Mabel taught piano lessons and Hazel had an art studio in their carriage house."

Barb looked at Estelle. "They introduced me to the world of art and music. You see, I was also what you'd call an 'odd bird.' "

"You followed in their footsteps, then," Gracie said softly.

"After their aunt passed on," Barb con-

17

tinued, "Hazel went back to New York, since collectors had begun buying her sculptures. Mabel followed to take care of her. They traveled all over the world but, still, always came home to Willow Bend."

"I remember their presentations at the library, with slides from the most exotic places. Really, who around here takes a vacation to the rain forests of Guatemala? And women going off on an African safari back then was pretty unusual, too."

Marge smiled at Barb. "I admired them, even if I never knew them as well."

"I say we give Hazel the biggest and best home-going birthday bash this church has ever seen!" Rick interjected. "Mabel's gone to be with the Lord, and that's something to celebrate."

A murmur of affirmative sounds came from the other choir members who were still lingering nearby and had stopped to listen.

"It would have to be approved by the church board," Estelle cautioned.

Marge grinned. "Several of them sing with us, remember? So I don't think that's going to be a problem."

"We could do a musical presentation," Rick suggested. "A stroll down memory lane, if you will."

"Sounds like a hit!" Pastor Paul had en-

18

tered the room and now joined the discussion. He smiled at her with affection.

As possible plans were being discussed, Paul took Gracie aside. "I think God put you in the right place at the right time to orchestrate a miracle." He smiled at her with affection.

Gracie didn't understand his meaning and lifted an eyebrow quizzically, waiting for him to continue.

What he told her was surprising: It seemed that Hazel and Mabel's uncle, Horace Rohleder, had provided well for his nieces. But, eventually, when they died, the full principal was to be released to the town to be used in projects that would benefit the community culturally.

"Willow Bend is the final inheritor of the estate," Paul told her. But there was a look of concern on his face.

Gracie failed to understand what the problem was. Since Hazel was still alive, matters need only continue as they were.

"The problem is not with Horace's estate — not directly, anyway. Mabel apparently died intestate, meaning she didn't have a will — although Hazel is sure she did." Paul went on, still looking troubled. "I think so, too, because she'd told me as much, before she was starting to fail."

He explained that he had also spoken to the lawyer handling Horace's estate. Frowning, he shook his head.

"Hazel has received legal notice that Mabel's death requires a review of the inheritance she shared with her sister, as called for in the provisions of their uncle's will. So she's asked me to talk to Nick Kendrick, the young lawyer recently assigned to the estate."

Gracie tried to organize her thoughts. Here were two eccentric old ladies who had retired to Willow Bend to live in the family home. Mabel had been in the advanced stages of a degenerative disease. The pair had taken care of each other all of their lives, and now one was alone and faced with a potential onslaught of legal wrangles.

Gracie had been meaning to visit Hazel ever since Mabel's funeral. Now, she made up her mind to call on her the next day. Meanwhile, she would pray.

Pastor Paul ran his fingers through his hair. Gracie noticed wisps of gray at his temple, and that he was in need of a haircut. Eternal Hope was an active congregation, and his flock struggled, like most people, with the problems of raising families, building marriages, putting bread on the table, and getting older. She sent another silent prayer heavenward on her pastor's behalf.

"There's a further problem," he sighed. "Toward the end, when I would go to visit, Mabel often talked about her wishes for funeral arrangements. I would listen, and she seemed at peace.

"One day, that suddenly changed. She brought up the subject of her estate. She was quite agitated — not with me, but definitely about something. What it was, she didn't say. But, then again, she wasn't quite making sense. I knew she had been prescribed a stronger pain medication. She rambled on about writing things down for protection. And that it was her wish that Eternal Hope benefit in her will.

"She kept saying that she trusted me, and to please take care of her sister. Then, Hazel came into the room, and Mabel began to ramble about childhood games. Out of nowhere, she asked Hazel to finish a sculpture she'd put aside years earlier, insisting that she get started on it immediately.

"With Hazel there, though, Mabel didn't seem to want to discuss her will, and I respected her need to handle things between them. So I didn't press her." Paul shut his eyes. "Mabel left us a few days later."

Gracie waited patiently for him to finish.

21

"Now Hazel appears reluctant to deal with estate matters. The lawyer, unfortunately, has already implied to me she might not be capable of handling her sister's estate. The grief she's feeling certainly seems natural to me, but for some reason, he's not factoring that in."

"So what can I do to help?" Gracie asked.

He looked embarrassed for an instant. "The problem is the lawyer apparently has pegged me as a con man, someone trying to swindle an old lady out of her money. He told me it's his job to protect her."

Gracie was indignant. "You're the most honorable man I know!" Paul blushed, his face bright pink under his sandy thatch of hair. He looked at her gratefully.

"As I see it," Paul went on, "the Rohleder twins had few expenses. I don't think they even often drew money from the estate funds, and they've completely trusted the firm that administrates the estate."

He explained that the lawyer who had originally set up the life estate providing for them was long deceased, and that it had practically taken care of itself all these years.

"Until this new fellow came to town, that is. Kendrick's, for some reason, taken a particular interest in it. They had several letters from him requesting a review of the terms of the estate. And now with Mabel's death — well, it's a lot for any elderly woman to handle, let alone one in mourning for a beloved sister from whom she'd been virtually inseparable. I'm reluctant to get in the middle of things. I certainly don't want to be accused of manipulating someone. At the same time, I care about Hazel and feel she needs my support."

Gracie remembered how difficult it had been for her after her husband Elmo died. Thankfully, her son Arlen had been there for her. He'd stepped into his father's shoes with ease. What was more natural than for Hazel to lean on her pastor?

"When I talked to Kendrick, he suggested Hazel sell the family property and move to one of those nursing homes that provides independent living accommodations. But he doesn't seem to understand. Hazel loves that house, and she'll never give it up."

Gracie was thoughtful. "Of course. And it's far too soon for anyone to put pressure on her."

"The truth is, we need prayer, Gracie — lots and lots of prayer. But I also need support. That's why I came to you. I don't want anyone ever to think I'm taking advantage of my flock."

"You aren't! You couldn't!" Gracie's eyes

flashed. She and the entire Eternal Hope congregation all adored their young pastor.

"I just want to save Hazel embarrassment. Whatever we can do to protect her dignity. . . ."

"I understand. You can count on me."

2

Uncle Miltie — aka George Morgan — was waiting for Gracie, his niece, after choir practice. His nickname had been bestowed because he reminded folks of Milton Berle, the once and not-quite-forever TV comedian. Now, it appeared that Willow Bend's own Uncle Miltie was passing on his tradition to a new generation of irrepressible punsters.

The Eternal Hope Youth Fellowship was busy with a project for their latest fundraiser in the communal kitchen, so the parking lot was active. Uncle Miltie had apparently seized the opportunity to show a young pal named Kevin Huling his new book of jokes, a gift from Arlen, Gracie's son.

Kevin was a boy who often had difficulty, Gracie had observed, finding his place among his peers. He had a tendency, sometimes, to go on without regard for his listeners. That made him a good disciple for her uncle!

Now Marge Lawrence called out to Gracie from her car. Gracie knew that her neighbor and best friend was bursting with curiosity about what she'd been discussing with Pastor Paul. But Marge said instead, "I've just had a great new shipment of stuff at the shop. Why don't you drop by and look at it?" Gracie was an infrequent visitor to her friend's gift shop, since she saw her so often in her own cozy kitchen.

"Okay. I need to find a birthday gift for Arlen."

"How is he? And his family?" Don Delano asked, as he opened his car door.

Gracie was happy to tell him about her grandson little Elmo's new fascination with birds and bird-watching, which he did with his parents in New York's Central Park. Of course, she also just happened to be carrying a miniature album of recent snapshots, a gift from Wendy, her daughter-in-law.

Uncle Miltie loudly cleared his throat, eyes twinkling, eager to catch his niece's attention. He looked conspiratorially at Kevin.

"We've got a good one for you!" Uncle Miltie chortled.

Kevin assumed the role of the straight man, watching his mentor with all seriousness.

"A fellow goes to a dermatologist with a

puzzling skin ailment. *'Hmm,'* the doctor says, 'try a milk bath.' So the guy walks into the supermarket and tells the manager he wants enough milk to take a bath. 'Okay, but do you need it pasteurized?' "

Kevin couldn't resist: "Past-yer-eyes," he repeated, emphasizing each syllable.

" *'Nah!'* the customer says. 'Up to my chin should do it.' "

The two of them slapped hands. Don chuckled politely as Gracie waved her uncle into the car.

"Wait, wait! We've got another one." Uncle Miltie held up a cautionary forefinger. "Did you hear what happened when the red boat and the blue ship collided?" he asked.

Kevin knew his cue. "No! What happened when the red boat and the blue ship collided?"

"They were marooned!"

Kevin's mother Sharon Huling came up behind them. "Hi there! Mind if I kidnap your sidekick here? Kevin tells me you're helping him work on a routine for the school talent show."

"Next stop, prime time!" Uncle Miltie boasted.

Gracie looked at him with affection.

"Well, I for one," Don told Kevin, "like a

27

guy with a sense of humor. It makes studying atoms and chemical reactions a lot more interesting."

Pleased, the boy couldn't help but smile. Don was a well-liked teacher who enjoyed a good laugh, even at his own expense. That was a rare quality for almost anyone, but especially for a faculty member.

Kevin's mother now reminded him he still had schoolwork to finish. Kevin explained that Uncle Miltie was helping him with a history project on World War II and that he'd done his research by interviewing the veteran.

It was clear God had made a difference in many lives by inspiring Pastor Paul to match Eternal Hope's older and younger members. Gracie herself had been partnered with Amy Cantrell, who was already a dear friend. They were both generous souls more likely to offer than to take, but Gracie knew sometimes Amy needed extra confidence and encouragement.

Marge had at first wanted to trade in her partner, young Jeffrey Larson. A whiz at computers, he had succeeded in creating a database of her store's entire inventory. This splendid accomplishment — a real boon for a small shopkeeper like Marge — quickly made her change her mind. Now the two of them were fast friends.

Yes, Gracie was convinced this new endeavor was a heavenly endeavor. It not only brought people together, but gave them fresh perspectives and all with God's blessing.

Sharon remembered to thank Gracie for having shared a recipe for carrot cake. "I tried it out for a neighbor's anniversary and they loved it!"

The Huling family had not been in Willow Bend long, and had worshipped at Eternal Hope for only a few weeks. Gracie understood the father worked on Sundays, but she was praying to see the three of them attend together some day soon.

"We've always been newcomers," Sharon told her. "This is really the first place we've lived that I've wanted to be more." She smiled at Uncle Miltie. "You've been wonderful to Kevin."

"He's a good kid to put up with an old duffer like me."

"Kevin doesn't really know his grandparents. They live at opposite ends of the country. My mom and dad are in Florida, and Dave's mother lives in Arizona. This partner program is good for him. Having someone like you take an interest means a lot."

Uncle Miltie, as he often did when touched, turned to humor. "I want him to have everything I didn't have when I was a kid — like passing grades, for instance!"

Kevin blinked. Then he grinned sheepishly.

His mother eyed him. "Schoolwork's not as much fun as learning new jokes."

"Kevin did a fine job interviewing me about my wartime service." Gracie, listening, knew how reluctant her uncle was to recall many of the awful things he had experienced as a soldier. But, for Kevin, he had made an exception.

"History's the only subject he does really well in. Mr. Morgan, do you think you could get him to take more of an interest in math?"

"Hey, Mom!" Kevin pleaded. "We've only lived here a few months. These teachers are a lot harder."

His mother took a longer view. "I told you to ask for some help, or else invite a friend home to study with."

"These kids have been together forever. It's not like you can just be instant buddies!"

Uncle Miltie broke in. "I'm no math whiz, but bring your books by tomorrow, Kevin, and we'll take a look at the assignment. Afterward, we can work on those new gags."

"*New* gags?" Gracie looked skeptical. "I noticed that that anthology features jokes used by the late Mr. Berle."

"*Hmmph!*" Uncle Miltie snorted. "Remember, my girl, like fine wine, jokes get better with time."

Sharon Huling hugged her son. "Your dad thought he'd be home early this evening, so we'd better get going."

"He's never home early." Kevin contradicted her.

Sharon ignored him. "Thanks again, Gracie — and Mr. Morgan."

They watched mother and son pull out of the parking lot.

"He's a good boy. But there's a sadness there."

"I can tell." Gracie held his cane while he slid into the seat. He grinned up at her. God did indeed have a knack for bringing the right people together, she thought as she closed the door for him.

On the way home, Gracie told her uncle what Pastor Paul had confided. His insight and his discretion were both qualities she valued; her uncle could be serious when the occasion called for it.

"I don't know Hazel Rohleder well. She's a quiet one, but sometimes at the senior center, she lets loose with a comment that's a reminder of all that she's seen and done."

Gracie glanced at him. "She's had an amazing life."

Uncle Miltie nodded. "A good person to have in your camp if you're taking on a fight, too, it seems to me."

"So, you think she can handle this problem with the estate?" Gracie asked.

"It's not a problem, yet — at least not from what you've told me. I think Paul's wise to put some distance between himself and the handling of the estate. But if I know you, my dear, you're going to be over there tomorrow."

Gracie laughed. "I do want to pay her a visit. I never really knew the Rohleder twins very well. Now that Mabel's gone, I feel a little guilty about that."

"There are only so many hours in the day, Gracie. Don't be hard on yourself. If I guess correctly, God is using you right now. You're going to know Hazel Rohleder a *lot* better before all this is resolved."

Gracie sighed, and her uncle continued. "She's grieving mightily now, but she'll handle this when she can't avoid it any more. It was the same with me, and with you, too. Legal concerns, unfortunately, don't go away just because you're still mourning your loss."

Gracie understood all too well how much energy grieving took. She hadn't wanted to deal with life, either, after El had died. And she'd had her son at her side. Not only did Hazel have no one to lean on, but one man, at least, seemed out to confound the process, demanding of her what, at the moment, was difficult to give.

"I hope you're right. This lawyer sounds determined. Pastor Paul isn't so confident."

"He's been put in a tough position. However, we know he's got prayer on his side — and you, my dear. You're the best advocate anybody could have." Gracie could feel her uncle's smile.

"Hazel needs her own lawyer. Someone without an interest in her uncle's estate. That's one practical thing you can advise her to do. And, in the meantime, we'll all get to praying. Aren't you always the one who tells us to trust God?"

They slipped into a comfortable silence. *Lord, thank You again for sending him to me.* First things first: She needed to hear Hazel's side of the story. Her niece, Carter Stephens, was an attorney and had recently helped her update her will and organize all the paperwork. Even though Carter worked in Chicago, Gracie could always call and ask for her reading of Hazel's situation.

Uncle Miltie groaned suddenly and sank deeper into his seat. His back must be giving him pain. Why he wouldn't take the medication the doctor prescribed, she didn't know. He was a tough old bird, stubbornly independent, and she had to respect him for that. But Gracie couldn't help wishing there was something she could do to make him feel better.

"You okay?"

"My years are sneaking up on me, that's all."

"You've had a long day." She quietly lifted her adored companion to God. *You know he's in pain, Lord. Even though he hates admitting it, he needs help managing it. Talk to him, Father, convince him to take it easier, and to use his medication when needed.*

"Rocky picked me up right after you left," he said, quickly changing the subject. "He promised to get that stuff I ordered for the shed."

Although Gracie had tried to dissuade him from tackling the renovation of her garden shed, her uncle insisted on "earning his keep." In his active years, back in Pennsylvania, he had been a successful contractor.

Working with tools was a type of worship to her uncle — and had been to her husband, too, for that matter. They both hammered out anger, sanded down resentments and painted over disappointment, their love of building things allowing them to draw closer to God. Gracie understood, since, when she was immersed in her cooking, she always felt refreshed and nearer to her Maker.

"A good night's sleep," Uncle Miltie told her. "That's all I need. I'll be fit as a fiddle tomorrow. Rocky's coming over first thing. We've got those cabinets to hang."

"They can wait." She shot him a stern look. "That garden shed has been a mess for a quarter century. A few more days, or even a week, won't matter."

Uncle Miltie grunted.

"Really, organizing the shed simply isn't a high-priority item!" She reminded him, "Anyway, that shed was El's domain, and the clutter never seemed to bother him."

"But El wasn't a contractor with nothing to do but be useless."

"Please! Useless is the last thing I'd ever call you!"

Her uncle and his wife had enjoyed a relationship not unlike hers and El's. Losing Aunt Doris to cancer had been hard on him.

Then, what had begun as a temporary visit to his niece had turned into a mutually beneficial living arrangement.

"You're indispensable. I don't know what I would do without you!" She looked at him fondly.

"That's what I tell Gravino." Uncle Miltie managed a chuckle. "He'd starve without me to help him find excuses to show up here at mealtime! But he also needed an excuse to buy that jigsaw we saw on sale. Now I have to teach him how to use it!"

Rocky Gravino had settled in Willow Bend after his wife's death, taking the opportunity to own and run the local paper. In the small Indiana town he'd found a home, one that was large in every way but size. He and Uncle Miltie loved to tease each other and sing Gracie's praises, equally. They also both enjoyed hearty appetites and the chance to exercise them on her tasty meals.

She changed the subject back again.

"Did you take your pain medicine?"

She knew he hadn't, and he confirmed it with a grunt.

"There's no sense in suffering, especially when you've been prescribed medicine to relieve it. The doctor's on your side." She chose her words carefully. "And, uncle dear, it is *just* strong aspirin — nothing addictive."

"I've heard of folks getting addicted to aspirin." He closed his eyes against a spasm. "And a person can't be too careful, you know. They tamper with bottles."

Frustrated, she sighed. "I guess a person can become addicted to almost anything. But take the pills, Uncle Miltie, for both our sakes."

"All right," he said, giving in sooner than usual. "I'll swallow a couple when we get home."

She wasn't going to let him off the hook. "I've got a water bottle and a few of your pills right here, as a matter of fact." She motioned for him to look in her purse.

"There's a big checkers competition coming up at the senior center, and qualifiers start tomorrow. I plan to take away first prize! I've been practicing up with Kevin. Even got a couple of new moves from the kid, proving that an old dog can learn a few new tricks."

Gracie chuckled. "I never doubted it. You're so good with him. He really respects you."

"He's lonely, I'll say that. No brothers or sisters. His dad's a salesman for some company out of Chicago, so he isn't around a lot. The mother has just gone back to work full-time."

Gracie didn't know much about the family. They were new to town, and like so many of the younger citizens she met, they hadn't made church activities a priority. She'd seen the change over the years at Eternal Hope: fewer and fewer members were involving themselves in fellowship activities. Sports camps and specialty classes were replacing Vacation Bible School, as well as youth activities.

"A penny for your thoughts," her uncle remarked as they turned into their driveway.

Gracie sighed. "Just thinking, that's all. Things do change."

"Time doesn't stand still, Gracie, not even in Willow Bend."

"Hazel and Mabel were self-sufficient when they moved back. Mabel's gone now, and there's some question about whether Hazel can take care of herself." She glanced at her uncle. He had already heard this from her just minutes ago, but he sensed this telling had another meaning, one closer to home.

Gracie, pulling to a halt, turned to face her uncle.

"This lawyer may challenge Hazel's competency to handle her sister's estate, and, ultimately, her own affairs. Estelle, for one,

38

thinks she can't handle them *now*. But how does anyone really know? A woman's future seems to hang in the balance, based on what *other* people think."

He looked at her.

"Someday, will someone challenge my ability to make my own decisions? Arlen has power of attorney, but he lives so far away. His world is so different. Will he appreciate my position? Understand my passion for this neighborhood, this home — my desire to remain connected to my church family? Or will he insist that I can't live alone? Will he force me to go to New York to be nearer to him?"

Uncle Miltie understood. His own children had wanted their father to live with them, but he had opted for independence. He'd chosen to stay with Gracie because with her he could be his own man, holding on to his freedom. He would not have been happy living in a condo with his busy middle-aged children. Here, the way Gracie needed him — and he, her — was a study in easy harmony.

"Arlen's your son, Gracie. He grew up in Willow Bend, and buried his dad here. I think if he thought about it, his heart would tell him the right thing to do."

He chuckled softly. "You're a young

woman yet. Wait 'til you're as creaky as me."

She laughed. "You're only creaky when you get stubborn about your medicine!"

"Well, being over the hill is a darn sight better than being under it!"

"Agreed!"

They relaxed in the easy intimacy of the moment.

"We've only got today, so don't fret about tomorrow. I'm thankful for that. I don't *want* to know if I'm not going to get up in the morning. This day, each day, belongs to God, and that's all I need to know. I wake up in the morning, pull these weary bones to a sitting position, and when my foot hits the floor, I thank Him for another day. That's how it is when you've put in your four score — you can't expect more. You develop a deep, abiding appreciation for the opportunity to love and be loved."

He paused and smiled. "Hazel knows that feeling. She's had a full measure of days. But God's given her more, so I figure He's got something planned for her, just like He does me." He reached for his cane, preparing to get out of the car.

"You'll help her realize that. You and Rocky and Marge. Just like all my friends back home did for me after Doris died. I really didn't want to go on without her. But I was convinced to stick around a while longer."

"I love you." Gracie regarded her uncle with more than an ordinarily affectionate gaze.

"Now, don't go all mushy on me."

"What do you say we savor the moment with ice cream? Tomorrow may not be certain, but I'm fairly sure today we've got hot fudge sauce and maraschino cherries."

"How did you know I'd been having chocolate dreams for the past couple of hours?"

"I knew because you're always having chocolate dreams. The trick is to indulge them without waking up with chocolate nightmares!"

"I thought I was the one who made the jokes around here!"

3

Gracie returned from her early morning prayer-walk, setting her little portable cassette player on the table. What had begun years earlier as grief management had mellowed into a very special time she shared each day with the Lord. As she strode through the streets of Willow Bend and the surrounding countryside, she often talked right out loud to God, voicing her concerns about friends and neighbors passed along the way.

The house was quiet except for the rhythmic ticking of the mantel clock. Uncle Miltie was already gone. Rocky had come and picked him up to take him to the annual sale at the home improvement center near Avery. No matter how she might protest, a renovated garden shed was in the making.

She hit the playback on the answering machine. The first message was from Barb Jennings, and Gracie promptly returned her call.

"I'm ashamed of myself, Gracie. I was

really too short with Estelle. I overheard her talking, and I should have ignored it. She'd been complaining about my choice of music, implying for the umpteenth time that I deliberately ignore her superior talent. So, I was already on slow boil and couldn't help myself. Now that I've cooled down, I want to talk with her about it. The trouble is, I know it'll just make her angry."

Gracie prayed aloud with the choir director. "Lord, give Barb words that heal rather than hurt. Help her to see in Estelle what You recognize. Give both of my friends wisdom and the patience to mend the tear in their relationship."

"Thank you," Barb said. "It's what I need to take strength from. But I need, also, to ask you something. It's in the wind that Eternal Hope stands to inherit a lot of money — I heard it at the ecumenical choir meeting. Now, I don't know much about this, but I sense trouble. Did Mabel Rohleder really change her will and give Eternal Hope everything destined for the town after Hazel's gone?"

"I don't know how to answer that," Gracie said honestly.

Barb paused. "Forgive me for being nosy, but I noticed you and Paul having a serious conversation. He's being implicated as the one behind the change in the will. As I hear it, up 'til now Willow Bend has been in line to inherit money for special projects — scholarships and the like."

"It sounds like idle gossip is keeping a lot of folks awfully busy." Gracie closed her eyes, silently praying for guidance.

"That's what I thought, and I said as much. I just wanted to hear it from you. I'd hate to think our church has caused problems in the community."

Gracie decided truth was the best cure for rumor. "All I know is that Paul visited Mabel just before her death, and she told him she wanted to bequeath Eternal Hope something. He's just not sure what. The lawyer is being suspicious, the way lawyers always are. I know Paul's feeling the strain of being put in the middle, so I'm sure he'd appreciate our prayers and support."

"He already has mine."

Gracie explained that, to the best of her knowledge, Mabel somehow had neglected to make a will. Because that was the case, the court would need to appoint an administrator.

"Hazel's the natural choice, since she's Mabel's only living relative. We'll just have to wait and see what happens."

Barb countered, "But Mabel did have a

will. At least that's what she told me. She said she wanted me to have the harpsichord. I didn't think about it being a problem, when Hazel called and reminded me of the bequest. So, there *must* be a will."

But where was it?

Gracie had just hung up when Comfort Harding called. The young mother had suddenly taken sick and had left her daughter with Hazel Rohleder, who lived close by. Comfort described her condition as overall achy, with no specific symptoms. "I haven't been feeling myself for a few days. You know how it goes: Kids pass on a million germs, but moms can't be sick. So I just keep going." Comfort was also a staff member at Keefer Memorial Hospital.

"How can I help?"

Comfort had dropped off Lillian at Hazel's house about an hour earlier. "She says they're fine together, but I'll rest easier if you could check in on them. I called Rick, and he can pick her up at the end of the afternoon. Hazel's housekeeper is there now, so I think everything's okay, but Hazel says Kathleen has a class later this afternoon."

"I'd planned to take Hazel some of my homemade lemon curd, anyway."

"Oh, she'll love that! She and Mabel

adored having tea parties. It's been so convenient, being able to leave Lillian there at a moment's notice. The two of them have been like special aunts to her!"

Gracie promised to phone Comfort with a report. "If only lemon curd was a cure for grief!"

"I know," Comfort agreed.

Rick's wife juggled parenting and work with what seemed ease, but she had a great deal of responsibility as a nurse anesthetist at the hospital. "There's no one to cover my shift tonight, but barring an emergency, it should be okay."

"I suspect you'll feel better after some rest, but it's not good to push yourself, dear. I could keep Lillian overnight, you know."

"No, it's all right, really. Rick loves playing Mr. Mom. He's going to pick up soup, and they'll serve me dinner in bed."

Gracie assured her she'd take Lillian home if Rick was running late, or couldn't make it. "Now, get some rest, dear. Everything's under control."

She punched Hazel's number. The older woman's voice seemed cheery. A child was usually the best medicine for an ailing heart.

"How are you, Hazel? I've been praying for you."

Gracie heard a sigh. "Grief comes and

goes. It's easier if I keep myself busy."

Gracie explained that she knew Lillian was visiting Hazel.

"We've pruned and watered the houseplants," said Hazel. "She helped me in the outside garden, too. We picked raspberries, and now we're going to make some jam."

"She's a darling!"

"Of the two of us," Hazel now said, "Mabel was always the more outgoing one. I appreciate how patient everyone's being with me. It's hard . . . just at the moment."

Gracie assured her that everyone understood. Her friends cared about her, and would welcome her whenever she felt comfortable rejoining the world beyond her loss.

"I'll be back at church soon, but I don't think that I'm up to it just yet. It's too many people all at once. I've had so many notes and cards and phone calls . . . and I appreciate them all."

"It's hard to move on," Gracie agreed. "You probably feel like you're betraying Mabel's memory by continuing with life. But you know that's not true. Our loved ones want us to go on enjoying to the fullest."

"We were sisters and best friends. There were few memories we didn't share. I can't make a cup of tea without thinking of her. She was so much a part of me. . . ."

Gracie prayed silently for God to be with her. After El's death, the choir at Eternal Hope had made all the difference to her. They'd put their arms around her, guiding her back where she belonged — in the choir loft, praising God. Now it was Gracie's turn to give sustenance.

"May I call you from time to time? Marge and I would love to include you in our plans."

"I fear I'm not good company."

"Grief will ease into memories. And those memories will grow sweet. Your friends will help you through, Hazel . . . if you let us."

"You already have, dear."

Gracie imagined she could feel Hazel's heart lightening — if only for an instant. *Thank You, Lord.*

"I know Comfort creates reasons to have me baby-sit for an hour or so on a regular basis. Barb checks on me, and Pastor Paul. I do feel blessed, Gracie, to have you all."

"Which brings me back to the other reason I called you in the first place," Gracie said. "I was hoping to drop over this afternoon."

"Do come over, please, Gracie. Lillian will be delighted to see you, as will I."

"Any time you prefer?"

"Kathleen's still here, but she has to leave early this afternoon to get to Avery in time for her evening classes. Whenever is fine."

Gracie remembered the young woman who provided personal care services in exchange for room and board. Kathleen Bailey was studying for a nursing degree at a nearby community college. The exchange had seemed a perfect solution to the problems of Mabel's failing health, and Kathleen's moving in had allowed Mabel to stay at home right up until the end, with help from a hospice organization.

Gracie now stretched to open the back door. Her large orange cat had joined her that morning on her prayer walk but had taken a detour to avoid his arch-nemesis, the neighborhood catbirds. They squawked and dive-bombed poor Gooseberry until he'd finally hightailed it back to the sanctuary of his own backyard. He was demanding entry now with a plaintive meow.

It was going to be difficult for Hazel to ask for help, Gracie knew, and she wanted to lay the groundwork.

"Is there anything I can pick up for you at the store on the way?" Practical help was a good way to begin.

"Kathleen's been already. No, I'm fine."

"I've been out walking, so I need a shower and to change my clothes. Then I should fix a little something for lunch for Uncle Miltie first, that's all."

Hazel laughed. "Lucky man!"

"I could bring over lunch — make a little extra, that is."

"We're having Lillian's special peanut butter and bananas on toast! But, thank you for offering."

"Then I'll see you in a couple of hours."

"We'll hold tea for you."

Gracie put down the phone. *Me and You, Lord. Lead me, and show me how to ease her burden.*

Gracie followed Hazel to the sun porch on the east side of the house. There were beautifully framed paintings and water-colors on every wall. Hand-blown glass and richly glazed pottery graced the tables. A music room featured a baby grand piano adorned with photos. The kitchen had been recently remodeled with new appliances.

On the sun porch, Lillian stood by a wicker table upon which sat an old-fashioned blue-willow tea service.

"This was Mabel's favorite room," Hazel said sadly. Then she remembered and brightened. "She loved to have friends for tea."

Gracie sat down on a wicker settee, patting the place next to her.

"My mommy's sick." Lillian climbed onto the flowered cushion beside Gracie.

Gracie hugged her. "She's getting her rest now and then she'll need lots of kisses. Are you going to be able to give her that medicine?"

Lillian nodded solemnly.

"Lillian's a wonderful cook," Hazel told Gracie. "Her banana-and-peanut-butter sandwiches are five-star!"

Lillian looked at Hazel. "I didn't know you could eat stars," she said wonderingly.

Hazel caressed the little girl's dark hair. "Well, I meant that your sandwiches are delicious!"

Lillian changed the subject, after beaming at Hazel's compliment. "Mommy helps people at the hospital. She helps them sleep so they won't have pain. Daddy says that's a very important job."

Gracie savored the warm sun streaming through the curtainless windows. Trays of African violets in pinks, purples and fuchsias on the windowsill were basking in the same. Lillian, giggling, was now biting a gingersnap around the edges, carefully reshaping it. "I'm making a star!" she announced.

It struck Gracie as interesting that this Victorian room also had on display contemporary works of art usually more at home with glass and chrome. A collection of marble shapes, with tunnels and soft curves highlighted in shades of pink, silver and a kind of mauve, graced the highboy. She knew these were Hazel's own sculptures.

"What do you think?" Hazel asked, catching Gracie off guard.

Gracie actually wasn't certain, and yet she wanted to be honest. "They're striking," she said, "and interesting, certainly."

Hazel smiled encouragingly.

"That's . . . all," Gracie told her. "Don't hold it against me!"

Now Hazel laughed. "It's all right, dear." Hazel put down the tray and looked at her visitor with affection. " 'Interesting' usually means you're baffled. But don't worry, you're in good company! Most people don't understand my work."

"I *do* like it — I just don't know exactly why."

"The 'why' isn't important, just remember that."

Gracie heard footsteps overhead.

"That's Kathleen. She's getting ready to leave for class."

"I really don't know her," Gracie admitted. "Does she have family in Willow Bend?"

"She doesn't talk much about them, but I know she lost her parents. Her father lived in Virginia, I believe. She has a stepmother and a brother. They weren't close, however. Her parents divorced when she was young, I take it not under the best of circumstances."

Gracie nodded and sipped her tea.

Hazel paused a moment to think, then shrugged. "I'm pretty sure she doesn't have anyone in the area. A couple of her friends have an apartment in Avery, and that's where she lived before joining us. Kathleen refers to herself as my personal care assistant, but I regard her as an angel of mercy. I don't know what I would do without her. She came to live here in exchange for helping us manage on our own."

Hazel bit her lip. "Forgive me, I still say *us*. I forget and start talking to Mabel, half expecting her to answer."

"I do the same thing with El," Gracie confessed.

Hazel looked over at Lillian. "We were so happy to be adopted by this lovely young lady. We've had such fun over the last few months, haven't we? At first, we began with tea on Tuesday, but lately, I've started baby-sitting on Saturday mornings. It was wonderful therapy for Mabel!"

"I'm not a baby," Lillian cautioned.

"No, you're not." Hazel agreed. "We're sitting each *other*."

"Sitting each other," Lillian repeated, giggling. "That's funny."

An old photograph of the sisters on a shelf caught Gracie's eye.

"It was our sixteenth birthday," Hazel explained. "Mabel wanted to have a big party, but things were still tight in those days. Uncle said we had to be careful — no extravagances, especially when others had so little."

"Your uncle and aunt raised you, I remember."

"Our mother and father died when Mabel and I were younger than Lillian. It was a terrible winter. Influenza. There were no medicines to stop it."

Hazel went on to explain that she and her sister had been raised by their uncle and his new wife, Leah. "My parents had been married late in life, and we were their double blessing. Uncle Horace often told us that. He and his brother had also been best of friends. My father and mother lived in this very house with them when they were first married."

"I didn't know that," Gracie said.

"It was big enough for all of us. My grandparents lived here, too, but they died when I was a little girl."

Horace had also married late in life, Hazel told them. Leah was the nurse who cared for his mother, so she had been with the family for a long time. "My grandmother was fragile, so Leah became a big part of our lives."

"It just seemed natural that they'd marry. We were happy when Uncle Horace married her. She was already a mother to us. He'd had an early marriage that didn't work out."

Lillian was listening intently.

"Uncle Horace was successful in his investments, and he adored us, so we were very spoiled. For her part, Mabel believed God gave us each other to make up for our parents' having gone to heaven so soon. But we also had Uncle Horace and Leah. It was a childhood as blessed as anyone could have."

"I heard you and Mabel had quite a big influence on Barb's life."

"I remember her in pigtails," Hazel reminisced. "She liked tea parties, too."

"We're going to have a *big* party!" Lillian reached for a ladyfinger. "A birthday party — for Miss Mabel, too."

Hazel turned to Gracie. "You will cater, my dear, won't you? I've been meaning to ask."

"Of course," Gracie replied. But there was still the question of whether the event would, in fact, be hosted by Eternal Hope. She decided not to mention any of the proposed plans.

"Birthday parties are fun!" Lillian said.

"That they are," Gracie agreed.

Lillian decided to retrieve her art box from her backpack to make a get-well card for her mother, promising to draw a picture for Gracie, as well. She spread the crayons and markers on the floor and stretched out on the floor. Before long, she was lost in concentration.

Gracie smiled, remembering her own son laboring by the hour to draw magic underwater kingdoms inhabited by brave knights on seahorses. Oh, for the gift of a lively imagination! How she had loved sharing with her own little boy his interpretations of his brightly colored creations.

"They grow up so fast."

"Indeed." Hazel was watching Lillian. "Mabel and I used to imagine ourselves as mothers. We loved fussing over Barbara. Her mother called us a godsend. Now, we say the same of Lillian. My sister never admitted it, but she was in a lot of pain for a very long time. Lillian arrived like a magic elixir, sweet as sugar and twice as invigorating."

Hazel suddenly became quiet, and Gracie recognized the undertow of grief. But it passed and Hazel changed the subject. "Now, tell me. What's going on in your life? And at church? I don't get out as much as I'd like, particularly when the weather changes. I'm afraid of falling, you know. I've made it this far with all my own parts, I don't aim to change that and end up with a hip replacement, like most folks around my age."

"I hope at your age I'm doing as well!" Gracie declared.

"It's not the physical ailments that get you down. I usually feel fine. But people seem to think I'm failing — that I don't know my own mind! They treat me like a child."

Lillian sat up, curious as to what this could mean.

"Some people think I need a baby-sitter, dear," Hazel told her.

"There you go, feeling sorry for yourself again." Kathleen appeared in the doorway. "Remember what Mabel said — you've got to get back into your work."

"Work?"

57

"I was humoring my sister." Hazel feigned a disapproving scowl at Kathleen. "I haven't done anything serious in years, nothing anyone would buy, anyway."

"What she isn't telling you is that there's a gallery in Chicago that wants to buy her sculpture," Kathleen told Gracie. "They'd like to feature Hazel's work in a special show, along with other artists doing similar work. She's known about it for a long time, but she keeps procrastinating."

Hazel protested, "You need steady hands to sculpt, and I don't have those anymore!"

"Your sister thought you did!" Kathleen was persistent. "She made me promise to keep after you about finishing it. Now I'm honoring that promise."

"I don't know —"

Kathleen cut her off gently. "Working in your studio makes you happy."

"My heart's not in it —"

"Mabel didn't want you pining away! Her words exactly."

Gracie reached out to touch Hazel's arm. "There's nothing wrong with your mind, my dear. And there's *certainly* nothing wrong with your heart. Let the two come together, and your hands will follow."

"Help me clear the tea table, please," Hazel now said to Lillian. "Why don't you carry out this little dish of cookies and have another while you're at it."

"Okay," Lillian obliged, her mouth already full of crumbs. She followed Hazel out of the room.

"So, what do you think?" Kathleen asked. "I worry that she's become even more forgetful since Mabel died. Today she seems alert, though — because Lillian is here. And happy, too. She was looking forward to your visit."

Gracie leaned back in her chair. "Grief is hard. I think she's reacting exactly as can be expected."

"But I can't help being concerned, especially when she gets confused. She slips back and forth into the past, and sometimes forgets what she's saying in the middle of a sentence."

Gracie pointed out, "Everyone suffers memory lapses as they get older. I wouldn't sell her short."

Kathleen looked unconvinced. "I don't want to. But I can't overlook what I see, and that's an increasing number of lapses. . . ."

There was a coolness about Kathleen that Gracie found disconcerting. Perhaps it was that she could not seem to look Gracie straight in the eye. Yet the young woman had chosen to seek a career ministering to the sick. And she obviously cared for Hazel. God had brought them together, Gracie was sure of it, just as He seemed to be using Lillian to ease Hazel's grief.

Kathleen glanced at her watch. "I'd better get going."

"I'll pray for you, dear, as I'm praying for Hazel."

Kathleen flashed a halfhearted smile. "I'm having a difficult time with organic chemistry. So I guess prayer couldn't hurt."

"Trouble will drive you to prayer, but prayer will drive away the trouble. That's what my mother used to say."

"Another Parks Family Rule?" Rick now stood before her, holding Lillian's hand.

Gracie chuckled. "No, but I could amend them to include one more."

"I didn't hear the doorbell," Kathleen said.

"I saw him out the window!" Lillian exclaimed.

"Before I could get out of the car, this little imp was in my arms."

Lillian leaned adoringly against her father's leg.

Rick went on to explain that Comfort had called him on his cell phone, and that she was feeling a little better. "My schedule is flexible, so I just headed on home to spend some time with my baby. She and I are going to cook her mommy dinner. They don't call me the Grill Master for nothing, you know."

Lillian corrected him, "I call you 'Daddy.' "

They all laughed.

"I'll bring over a casserole tomorrow," Gracie told him. "Even if Comfort's feeling better, a day or two of rest seems in order."

Rick thanked her. "She thinks it's some kind of virus. So any help's appreciated — especially when the offer includes something from the kitchen of Gracie Lynn Parks." She blushed.

"Lillian's an angel!" Gracie returned the compliment. Rick beamed proudly. "I don't get to see little Elmo enough, and, besides, I've always wanted a granddaughter."

"The best decision we ever made was to move to Willow Bend," Rick told Kathleen. "You have a hard time finding friends like this in the big city."

Kathleen simply smiled politely.

Gracie watched her and wondered what kept her from responding to Rick's infectious warmth.

Hazel appeared in the doorway with a tray. "Time for tea!"

61

"I really have to go." Kathleen pushed herself to stand.

Rick tried to excuse himself, but Hazel refused to take no for an answer. Gracie was puzzled to find the tea party starting over again, but Lillian seemed delighted.

"Barbara dear," Hazel smiled at her, "why don't you offer your father some cake."

"Ladyfingers!" Lillian was indignant. "And it's *Lillian!*"

"May I pour you tea?" Hazel asked innocently.

Kathleen turned to Gracie, as if to say, "See? I told you so."

Father, we need Your wisdom. Show us the best way to be of service to Hazel.

4

Gracie returned home to find Uncle Miltie in the backyard. Stretched over a pair of saw-horses were a pair of pine cupboard doors, and encircling him was his collection of power tools. Her darling uncle was in his glory, knee-deep in another home improvement project.

It had come about this way:

Gracie had happened to mention in passing the lack of organized storage space in the shed. That was the same day her uncle received the home improvement center sale flyer in the mail. Rocky Gravino had been there for dinner, and thus a new project was born.

Rocky's official job may have been editor and publisher of the local paper, the *Mason County Gazette*, but in his off hours he was as avid a do-it-yourselfer as anyone could hope to meet. The trouble was he was as stubborn as he was enthusiastic, and he and her uncle could spend the morning arguing over a single hinge.

Wedged in the corner of the shed, Rocky now had his back to her. He was working at tightening screws on the new cupboard's framework.

"What do you think?" Her uncle turned to greet her with a paintbrush full of shellac.

"Beautiful!"

He reached to turn off the portable stereo perched on a nearby bucket of bird seed.

"Thank goodness!" Rocky exclaimed. Turning around, he grinned. "Hi there!"

"Hi yourself!" Gracie replied.

Uncle Miltie beamed at both of them, then changed his expression to a mock-scowl. "Rocky here somehow managed to spill his coffee over the steel wool I handed him."

The newspaper editor shot a dirty look in the direction of Gracie's uncle. "Well, soggy steel wool may not be highly usable, but at the same time it's extremely replaceable. We're not talking priceless gems here."

"Gentlemen, please!" Gracie said, forcing back laughter.

"He's clumsy, that's all, and it wouldn't hurt him to be more careful."

"Uncle Miltie!"

"At least I'm no tattletale," Rocky commented under his breath.

Gracie just shook her head, recognizing

their bantering as the cement of friendship. Rocky adored her uncle, and the older man really treasured the younger's respect.

Gracie watched them work for a few minutes more, thanking God for this friendship. It was Rocky's no-nonsense style of encouragement that had helped her uncle through the hardest part of his grieving. His health had seemed to be failing then, and he had been starting to feel sorry for himself. Rocky had simply refused to tolerate it.

It was his offering to help with those small projects her uncle wanted to tackle that gave him the boost he needed. The next thing they knew Uncle Miltie had regained his sense of life . . . and humor.

"It looks great." She patted her relative's arm, then bestowed a kiss on his cheek.

"Thank me when my apprentice and I get the project finished."

Rocky rolled his eyes upward. Gracie grinned at him, then headed for the kitchen door.

"*En garde!*" Rocky held up his screwdriver like a fencing *epée*. Gracie stopped and waited to see what was coming next.

"I'll *en garde* you! Who cut the board twice and complained it was still too short?"

Rocky gave a helpless shrug. "It's a new tool — what can I say?"

"He's a fine carpenter. Really!" Uncle Miltie admitted, with a twinkle in his clear blue eyes. "For a newspaperman, that is."

"I'll have you know that I have to this day the wooden knife holder I made in ninth grade," Rocky said smugly. "And it's still in use."

Uncle Miltie couldn't resist the ready-made opening. "*Wow*, a genuine antique! Do you think we should pack it up and send it to the Smithsonian?"

"Be good, you two!" Gracie warned. "Or I'll send you to bed without any supper."

"That reminds me." Rocky wrapped his arm around his friend. "What's for supper?"

"Spaghetti pie."

"The best!" they said in unison.

"And lemon cake for dessert."

"*Uh oh,*" Rocky gulped, as Uncle Miltie blushed pink.

Gracie lifted an eyebrow.

Rocky grinned sheepishly. "That lemon cake was mighty fine, Gracie. You got lots of compliments."

"You guys ate it *all?*" She couldn't believe it. "Already?"

Her uncle turned defensive. "Roy and Lester and some other fellows stopped by. We needed some help hanging the frame."

"We needed a bribe," Rocky corrected him.

Uncle Miltie chuckled. "Didn't have to ask them twice."

"I did wash the pan for you, Gracie," Rocky said.

"Well, then it's plain old vanilla ice cream for you tonight."

"Come on, you've got to love us," Rocky coaxed as he pointed to their progress.

"Besides, we work cheap!" Uncle Miltie now positioned the other door to shellac.

Inside the house, Gracie called the Hardings to check on Comfort, but there was no answer. She glanced at the clock — almost seven.

"How's supper coming?" Rocky called as they were tidying up. "I'm famished!"

Her uncle bent to sniff the pasta dish cooling on the counter. "Why two casseroles, Gracie?"

She set a salad on the table. "I defrosted a second one for the Hardings. Comfort's under the weather. I'm going to take the unbaked one over to their house in the morning so they can have it for dinner tomorrow."

"That's right, you went over to Hazel Rohleder's to get Lillian," her uncle remembered. "What's wrong with Comfort?"

"Some sort of bug. But probably a short-lived one. She works so hard at the hospital, and has a family to take care of."

"How's Hazel doing?" Rocky asked.

"She misses her sister, which is to be expected, but physically, she seems great."

It was her turn to say grace, and Gracie took a silent extra moment to offer up an affectionate prayer for her cantankerous but lovable workmen. She felt very lucky to be so blessed.

Uncle Miltie dug into the spaghetti pie. "Hazel used to drop in at the center with her sister from time to time, but she was always the quieter one."

Rocky countered, "I actually had the opposite experience. I'd see Hazel out walking quite regularly, and she would always greet me. She'd have intelligent comments about the paper." He reached for the salad bowl.

"I believe Hazel has won several international prizes for her sculptures," Gracie told them. "Rocky, why don't you assign a profile of her?" Now that it had occurred to her, it seemed a perfect way to lift her spirits.

It had never seemed odd to Gracie that the sisters had chosen to retire home to Willow Bend. But, still, it was a big world out there, and Hazel had once had a distinguished artistic career. Why not remind everyone?

As she served dessert — chopped nuts

and fudge sauce atop the vanilla ice cream — she brought up the matter of the cloud hovering over Pastor Paul.

"People talk," Rocky said thoughtfully. "It's just the way it is. Especially in a small town. You know that. Most of the time one's wise not to pay much attention to it. But this time, I think your pastor is right. He does have cause for concern."

Gracie put her spoon down to listen.

"The council's been murmuring about that estate for years. Mabel's death has brought its existence — and its potential benefit to the town — front and center once again."

"We *are* using the interest, though," Gracie pointed out. "I've seen the line item on the budget."

Rocky nodded. "Even the interest is a hefty hunk of change, but it's nothing compared to the Rohleder principal."

Gracie was worried. "I hope Hazel isn't going to suffer on account of everyone's eagerness to access those funds."

"Money talks," Rocky told her. "Nick Kendrick's running for state assembly, and he's pushing his pet projects. For example, there's that business of developing the property on the edge of town. And he's not alone. Lot of folks stand to gain by it.

"The area needs a public access road, and water and sewage lines will have to be extended before any housing can go in. The town owns most of that land, but some of it's private. It can't be developed without that access road."

"Do you think Kendrick might do something dishonest to make it happen?"

Rocky began to reply but Uncle Miltie interrupted. "That's marshland! Who's going put a house out there? Cows don't even use it for pasture."

"Swamps can be drained," Rocky reminded him. "That land is centrally located along what they believe will be the corridor for the new highway."

He sighed. "Our mayor is also gung-ho on this project, and I wouldn't be surprised if Tom Ritter doesn't have a few fingers in the development pie. That land is strategically located to link Willow Bend and Avery to the cities beyond, and will open them up to future development. The Rohleder estate money could make it all happen. Quite a few people have reason to push to get that money turned over to the town, so it's not just Nick Kendrick who should concern us. I see him as ambitious, not a crook."

"I don't want Hazel getting swamped by all this civic fervor," Uncle Miltie said. "Her well-being obviously can't be of prime concern to those who regard her as being in the way of progress!"

Rocky eyed him over the rim of his coffee cup. "The problem remains that the estate is worth a lot of money!"

"It seems everyone's looking for the advantage," Gracie observed.

"Money, my dear, drives our society," Rocky reminded her. "Even here in idyllic Willow Bend. What else is new?"

"*Hmmph!*" Uncle Miltie snorted. "The question is, do we manage the money, or does *it* manage *us?*

"Money also drives politics, which is a powerful force in itself."

"There are honest politicians, particularly here in Willow Bend," Gracie told herself.

Rocky tipped his cup and smiled. "And we loved one of the best of them. El was an honorable politician and a good friend."

Gracie smiled. Rocky really was a wonderful friend.

"Still, a little healthy skepticism in this case isn't a bad idea," Rocky said, returning to the subject. "Nick Kendrick does have a stake in this, but so do a lot of other people, including a member of your congregation. Ed Larson's one of the speculators. He sells insurance, but dabbles in real estate."

71

Gracie thought about this bit of information as Rocky continued.

"Kendrick's the new administrator of the Rohleder estate, so he has the final say on how any money's spent. When he approves using it to do something for the town, it puts him in the limelight." Rocky smiled wryly. "Free publicity."

Uncle Miltie leaned back in his chair. "So, he's motivated to see that Hazel doesn't stand in the way."

Gracie's heart sank. Uncle Miltie was right, of course.

Rocky cautioned now, "Remember what I just said. Nick Kendrick's probably no swindler, merely a fellow with his eye out for himself. Politically speaking, that is."

"He's in charge of a large estate," Gracie reminded him. "Isn't that an obvious conflict of interest?"

Rocky shrugged. "Not if he can negotiate an equitable settlement."

"Hazel remains the obstacle," Uncle Miltie said.

"That's why we've got a town council. Your vote is the same as his. That's what democracy is all about."

Rocky finished his ice cream. "But you've got to face facts. Even sleepy little Midwestern towns aren't exempt from progress.

Kendrick may have settled here hoping to take advantage of our provinciality, but he's got to have a constituency. Lots of the new transplants here are for change. They want cineplexes, more big box stores, faster highways and so on."

Uncle Miltie looked positively mutinous. "They might want it, but that doesn't mean that we have to give it to them. I like Willow Bend just the way it is!"

"You and me both. But we have to be realistic. Nick Kendrick may not see the situation the same way you and I do, but that doesn't mean he's a bad guy. It's better to work with him than against him."

"So, what do you suggest that Hazel do?" Gracie wanted to know.

"Hazel isn't contesting her uncle's will. If Mabel wanted to give a gift to Eternal Hope, it should be honored. We just have to be careful not to confuse the two. That's where the gossip needs to be nipped in the bud. Mabel's estate does not affect Horace."

Rocky met her gaze. "Convincing people of that will be the challenge. It often doesn't matter what the facts are. It only matters what the people *think* the facts are. Right now, many of our fellow citizens believe the town's interests are being compromised."

"Hazel's the key," Uncle Miltie reasoned

73

out loud. "She needs to make the situation clear."

Rocky nodded. "You, Gracie, will do us all a big favor if you can help figure out a way to make that happen."

"Finding Mabel's will sure would solve everything," Uncle Miltie noted.

"It would certainly make it all much simpler," Rocky agreed.

"I think she had one." Gracie outlined what she knew. "The question is why she didn't make it known. Was it because she wasn't capable, what with medication and pain getting in the way? Or was it something else? We've heard Mabel was upset, but no one seems to know why. She also told people that she'd written a will. She was incoherent at the end, but was there something cryptic in her last conversation?"

Rocky pondered this.

"Someone should talk to Nick Kendrick," Uncle Miltie decided. "He's the one with access to all the estate documents."

Gracie saw quite well where the conversation was going. "And whom do you suggest should confront the issue?"

"Why, *you,* my dear," Uncle Miltie said.

"It always comes back to you," Rocky told her.

"I need to pray."

"It doesn't surprise me," Rocky said affectionately.

"If you'll excuse me," Uncle Miltie said, glancing at his watch, "the TV's waiting for my company!"

"Well, I'm happy to stay put and help clean up," Rocky announced. "And for what it's worth, I'm looking forward to the birthday party."

"On that score, I can tell you," Gracie informed them, "that Rick and Bert are talking to the church board at the next meeting."

Rocky grabbed a dish towel from a hook. "It's all going to work out."

"I hope you're right."

"Do you think she's incompetent?" Rocky eyed Gracie steadily.

"Absolutely not," she stated firmly.

"Nor do I." They both smiled.

"We're all getting older, my dear. Sooner or later we'll probably find ourselves facing a similar situation to what Hazel's going through."

"Let's just hope there's not an opportunist like Mr. Kendrick in the wings."

Rocky leaned against the counter. "There are always opportunists. The important thing is to stay the course."

"You're right. El used to say that no one

grows old by living, only by losing interest in living."

"He was right, as usual."

"People think this party is a crazy idea," Gracie admitted.

He smiled. "But you love it. Me, too."

She sighed.

"Hazel will be fine, Gracie."

"She doesn't have anybody."

He gave her hand a squeeze. "She's got you."

God had brought Gracie and Hazel together for a reason, she was sure of it. Was it to satisfy an old woman's wish for a birthday party? Or was it something more?

Lord, what is it You want me to see . . . ?

Gracie had just turned back the covers on her bed when the phone rang. She'd almost decided to let the machine get it, but a nudge came from deep inside herself. *Okay, Lord.*

"Gracie, it's Rick Harding."

She could feel the awful urgency in her friend's voice.

"Comfort's in the hospital."

"Oh, no!" She hung up the telephone and was down the stairs before she even realized she'd not asked a single question.

76

5

"She's okay," Rick reassured Gracie, who had thrown on her clothes and rushed over. "It was her appendix, but they got it in time. Thank goodness she was at work!"

Gracie listened as her friend detailed his wife's day. The flu-like symptoms had worsened, but Comfort had insisted on showing up at the hospital on schedule. She had no sooner punched in than she'd collapsed. "One advantage of working on the premises: she was prepped and ready for surgery by the time I got there."

"How's Lillian?"

"Sleeping. Amy came over when I got the call. I intend to go home in a little while."

Gracie recognized that his trust in the good Lord was underpinning his natural concern for his wife. Rick was one of those men whose faith was part of his strength. She hugged him.

"It sure scared me, Gracie," he told her gratefully.

Gracie bowed her head and prayed aloud.

"Lord, put Your arms around Rick, and comfort him. Be with his wife tonight as she rests safely here, and be with the nurses and doctors who attend her. Help Lillian to understand that everything's going to be fine. Surround this family with Your love, Father."

Rick's "thank you" for her prayer was heartfelt.

"We should both go home now. I'll come over first thing in the morning to help take care of Lillian."

"It's Sunday," he reminded her.

Gracie paused. "Will you come back before church? I can have Lillian ready for Sunday school, and we can meet in the sanctuary before worship. I'll call Hazel and see if she's ready to come back to church. Helping with Lillian might just be the spur she needs."

The choir loft buzzed with concern for Comfort. Rick assured them she was doing well, and was eager to see Lillian later that day. Marybeth Bower insisted the father and daughter have dinner with her family later that evening.

"Amy, could you baby-sit tomorrow after school?" Rick now asked their young soprano.

The blond teenager looked unhappy. "I'm sorry, but I have to work at the deli. Abe gets the weekly delivery of supplies on Mondays and he'll be too busy to take care of it all alone."

"How about me?" Gracie offered. "I'll pick her up at nursery school, and then we'll head for the park."

"Great." He looked gratefully at Gracie. "If I know my daughter, she'll jump at the chance to go to the park."

Barb now weighed in. "It's good to see Hazel in church. Thanks, Rick, for making her feel included in your family. I know she really appreciates it."

Hazel had actually been reluctant to come. It was only after Gracie had pled on Lillian's behalf that the elderly woman had given in.

Gracie pointed out that the child would have to sit by herself while she and Rick sang with the choir. Of course, that wasn't exactly the truth, since any one of the church families would have been happy to include Lillian. (Gracie had decided that her little deception was allowable since her goal was the worthy one of getting a needy soul back into the church family.)

Bert Benton grabbed his robe off the hook. "We'll discuss hosting the party at the meeting tonight."

"We know, and I'm sure they are going to approve it, since everyone's already talking about it." Marge had been listening and now contributed her piece. She added, "Now that Hazel's here, we'll hug the grief out of her."

Marge's hugs had once been a balm for Gracie's grieving heart. Gracie, herself, wasn't entirely convinced that Hazel was the huggable type, but if anyone could do it, it was Marge.

She smiled, recalling Marge's gift of a hair-coloring kit. That box of L'Oreal Tango Spice had represented Gracie's new lease on life, her friend had declared.

And, sure enough, she'd been right.

Kathleen Bailey greeted Gracie and Lillian at the door when they arrived the next afternoon to ask Hazel to accompany them to the park. "She's in her room."

The young woman made no effort to let them in.

Lillian piped up, "We want her to come with us."

"I don't know. . . ." Kathleen glanced back in the house. "She's been moody since returning from church yesterday. I am not sure she's ready for another outing."

"Well, it can't hurt to check with her, and see if she'd enjoy it." Gracie understood the young woman's desire to protect her charge.

Kathleen stepped back, motioning them toward the stairs. "First room on the right."

Gracie knocked on the door.

"I'm not hungry."

"It's Gracie."

"I'm not in the mood for company."

"We're going to the park!" Lillian sang out.

No response came.

Gracie leaned closer to the door. "Hazel, dear, Lillian would really like you to go. It'll help take her mind off her mother. Please! It'll be fun."

Gracie could hear movement in the room. "Hazel?"

"I don't move very fast."

"We'll wait for you in the living room."

"Is she coming?" Kathleen wanted to know when they got back downstairs.

Gracie nodded. "I think so."

"Hazel usually gets up at the crack of dawn. She always fixed breakfast for herself and her sister. Now, she sometimes spends half the day in bed." Kathleen glanced at Lillian. "Except when Lillian's coming. So you're probably right, a visit to the park will

81

cheer her up. It's a lovely morning, and she'll be glad once she's there."

"Grieving isn't easy," Gracie reminded Kathleen. "We each have to do it in our own time, and in our own way. I know you understand. Hazel told me a little bit of your history."

A spark of emotion lit the young woman's normally cool countenance. Gracie suddenly felt that there was something about this girl that the Lord wanted her to understand. "You're welcome to join us, if you like," she offered. "I packed plenty of lunch."

"No, I've got classes. But I'll fix Hazel's supper and put it in the refrigerator, so all she'll have to do is warm it up later on. I have a long class tonight and am going to stay in Avery with friends." Kathleen looked at Gracie with concern. "You'll remind her, won't you? I'm afraid she won't eat if someone doesn't."

"Of course I will, my dear."

From the stairway landing Hazel called out to them, "Did someone say we're going to the park? I want to be the first to push a swing!"

Lillian squealed, "Me! You can push me!"

Two young mothers greeted them from a

bench when they arrived at the park. Gracie didn't recognize either, and Lillian didn't acknowledge the pair of little boys in the sandbox nearby. When Gracie made small talk, she discovered both women were newcomers to the area. Hearing this, she invited them to church — but, sadly, neither seemed very interested.

Hazel helped Gracie spread the blanket in the shade. It surprised her how few children were in the park on this sunny day, particularly since school was out. But then, she supposed, it was to be expected, with so many mothers working outside the home these days. "It's kind of sad," she thought out loud.

"What is?" Hazel asked.

"I was just remembering how this park used to bustle with activity. There were lines for the sliding board. It was our social hub back then."

Lillian called out from the swing, which was near the bench where the two women were still chatting. Gracie walked toward her.

"I hear they have plans for renovations at the elementary school," the blonde told the brunette. "They're also planning to equip this park with better and safer equipment."

"That, at least, will be an improvement!"

The brunette's tone was terse.

Gracie tried not to eavesdrop.

"It could make a difference in attracting nice new families." The pretty blonde, dressed in jeans and a nicely tailored blazer, stood up to help her son dump a bucket of sand to add a wing to the castle he was building.

The brunette rolled her eyes. "It'll take a lot more than that. There's no decent housing in this area! My husband and I had a hard time finding a place when the bank transferred him to its new branch here."

"I suppose that's true. We were looking for a centrally located fixer-upper. And we wanted to live in a small town." She chuckled. "I guess I didn't realize how quickly it'd get claustrophobic. But Willow Bend *is* a good place to raise kids."

Gracie didn't agree about the claustrophobia, but, still, the blonde was on the right track.

"It'd be better if it had some decent shopping and more entertainment for the kids."

The blonde shrugged. "I suppose. But they're planning to develop some land on the edge of town, and that will at least provide some nice new homes."

"My husband says a lot of the diehard townies are dragging their feet on that.

They're afraid Willow Bend will change. Look more like Avery, heaven forbid!" She shook her head. "My mother calls it a provincial little backwater."

The blonde glanced toward Gracie and Hazel taking turns pushing Lillian. Her expression was apologetic.

"We were talking to a lawyer friend, and he thinks if Willow Bend's going to get serious about growing, they'll have to elect some more progressive people. My husband's encouraging Nick to run. He says the time's ripe for change."

The blonde stood up again to call her child. "It does seem to be stuck in a time warp. And, though I like living in a small town, I suppose you're right — we've got to push for change if we want it to grow."

The trouble, Gracie thought, was that growing wasn't entirely about size. Willow Bend, in its own way, was plenty big enough. For one thing, there was an abundance of friends and family who were there for you when you needed them. Life moved at a comfortable pace, illuminated by the beauty of nature's changing seasons. Gracie longed to get up and tell them that Willow Bend, in the words of her dear uncle, was the closest a person could get to heaven this side of the Pearly Gates.

Instead, she gave Lillian's swing a firm push. The little girl giggled with delight, and Gracie felt her momentary anger dissipate.

"Most people don't know what they want, but it's always something different from what they have," Hazel said to nobody in particular, but loud enough to be heard. She looked defiantly in the direction of the bench.

El had believed people needed to feel that they had been heard, that their opinions mattered. He had encouraged everyone to participate in the governing process. She smiled, thinking that he might even have voted for Nick Kendrick just for the sake of balance.

The blonde stood up for a third time, announcing that it was time to head home for lunch. She wished Gracie and Hazel a good day. "What time did you say that church starts?"

Gracie definitely liked this young woman, but, still, she would send up prayers for both families. She owed it to the future of Willow Bend. "We can't blame them for wanting what they think is progress," Gracie said after they left. "They have an investment in this town, too."

Hazel watched the young mothers herd

their children toward a silver minivan. "Uncle Horace used to say that coming together was the beginning, staying together progress, and working together success."

"What a splendid thought!" Gracie said and told her about the Parks Family's Five Rules to Live By. "The most important being this one: A dash of prayer helps any recipe."

Lillian demanded excitedly, "Let's do the sliding board now!"

Gracie glanced at her watch. "How about some food first?"

Lillian jumped to the ground to retrieve the picnic basket.

Hazel lowered herself onto the blanket. "At least Mabel's free of the aches and pains of old age. I can't help wondering why we go on after a body's outlived its usefulness."

"This will make you feel better." Lillian handed her a peanut butter sandwich.

Hazel stroked the girl's headful of tiny braids, fingering the beads that decorated the ends. "Thank you. I'm sure it will."

Children were certainly gifts from God, entrusted to parents for a short but precious time, thought Gracie. "Thank You, Lord, once again for the many wonderful blessings You've bestowed, especially for cherished gifts of the people in our lives," she said as they prepared to eat.

"Amen!" Lillian exclaimed.

Soon, Lillian was skipping off to introduce herself to a little girl just arriving at the sandbox.

"If we could only tap a fraction of that energy!" Hazel said, watching her play with her new friend.

Gracie agreed. "Exhausting and invigorating, all in the same adorable bundle."

Hazel smiled. "Thanks for including me! It's good to get out of the house."

"Fresh air for fresh thoughts."

Hazel drew a breath of it. "Just what I need. Kathleen was right: Mabel would hate to see me wallowing. I just can't seem to shake it, Gracie, and it's not all grief. That, I know. Mabel's with the Lord. Something just keeps me feeling down. Sometimes I don't want to go on. And then I feel terribly guilty."

What she was describing was the dark side of bereavement. Guilt lurked just beneath the grief — questioning, blaming and taunting. "You ask yourself why it wasn't you who died. Or if you could have done anything differently. You think you might have given more, listened more —"

"Loved more," Gracie finished for her.

Hazel nodded. "Lots of *if onlys*."

Gracie decided to counter this with a bit of sweet reasonableness. "Uncle Miltie pointed out the other night that we have our chance with every fresh sunrise. Losing someone makes the value of a day all the clearer."

Gracie now offered Hazel a piece of fruit. "That's why you need to reconnect with people. What is life for but to enjoy God and His gifts? And you can't do that unless you're involved with people."

"I'm not a 'people person,' " Hazel protested, "although I dislike that expression."

"You're with some now."

"You won't let me off the hook, will you?"

Gracie shook her head. "The thing is to get involved in something new. It not only eases the grief, but that way you'll have something to look forward to. It makes all the difference when you get that 'what's the use?' feeling. Taking on new challenges helped after El was killed. When I felt stuck, I pushed myself — with Marge's and everyone else's help — and I started a catering business."

"But there are still so many details to take care of." Hazel let out a long sigh. "I should have followed through on our wills. Mabel wanted me to, but I just couldn't face it after we got her prognosis."

She looked sheepish. "The truth is, we ignored such matters all our lives. Practicality went against the grain of my bohemian nature, and Mabel humored me in everything. She always handled the household matters, allowing me space to create. She took such pride in my work. It was as if we shared a single spirit."

Gracie reminded Hazel that Mabel had been an artist in her own right. "Barb says she was a wonderful pianist."

"Mabel would entertain our friends. She also played the harp and an old harpsichord my grandfather won in a bet. She could even play the harmonica! Though Uncle Horace's estate freed her to pursue her passion, music remained secondary to her, purely recreational. She was happiest taking care of us."

Gracie leaned back to enjoy the breeze and the smell of freshly cut grass. "It seems strange you never married."

"We got caught up in our freedom and our love of one another, and before we knew it we were old maids." She laughed. "Eccentric old spinsters is more like it. We didn't plan it that way, but we were never sorry, really. We had each other."

Gracie thought this over. It was so different from her own life.

"But now Mabel's gone, and I truly must see to her estate."

"If only she'd made a will," said Gracie.

Hazel told Gracie she had. "At least I think so. The medication had her confused some of the time, and one couldn't predict when. She was in quite a strange mood the day she had me call Paul. I told her that I'd phone the lawyer handling our family affairs, but she insisted that I call the pastor — which I did, and you know the rest. She told him that she had one, but I didn't see it. Then or now. I've looked everywhere."

Gracie broached the inevitable. "Perhaps you should talk to Nick Kendrick."

"What am I going to say? I don't know where that will can be. I'd feel so stupid and incompetent, I'd be proving his suspicions about my competency. No, I don't want to talk to him. I'll deal with it in my own time."

Gracie touched her arm. "But you don't have time. Someone will have to take charge and the court will appoint an administrator. You should take the initiative. You're the logical candidate for administrator."

"I tried to make sense out of the papers sent by the lawyer's office, but I can't. It frustrates me. Really, Gracie, I can't always concentrate. I sometimes lose track of time. Quite frankly, when I'm nervous or upset, it gets worse. I'm *afraid* to talk to him."

Her eyes filled with pain. "Everyone knows I get disoriented. I can't hide it. If I'm just left alone, I can calm down, and then everything's fine. But start prodding and questioning, and I panic. I can't even think."

"You managed to care for Mabel every day." Gracie met her gaze. "Kathleen said you fixed her breakfast every morning. Then you were capable of doing what needed to be done. So, now, if you feel yourself panic, pray. Before you go see Nick Kendrick, pray. I'll be praying."

Hazel looked away. "Mabel didn't trust him."

"Who, the lawyer?"

"I'm not sure, but she made me promise to be careful."

What could this mean? Gracie wondered. It seemed that a moment was drawing near when she would have to meet Nick Kendrick and decide for herself.

"Come here!" Lillian suddenly shouted, and the two women, in obedience, rose slowly to their feet.

"We're on our way," Gracie called.

6

When she got home, Gracie saw the flashing light on her answering machine. There were three messages.

The first was from Barb, telling her that the birthday party had been approved.

The second message was from Arlen. She would call him back after supper when rates were cheaper, and she'd have more time to enjoy the conversation with her son and his family.

The third sounded urgent. She punched in Paul's number on the portable phone.

At first, the pastor made small talk, and Gracie let him ramble on, until it became quiet on the other end.

"After I left that message," he began, "I realized I was blowing this way out of proportion."

She sat down. "What, Paul?"

"One of the pastors in the ministerium took me aside today. He said he'd heard what he hoped was idle rumor. It's going around that Eternal Hope has received several large bequests, and that I orchestrated them in order to look good to the board."

"Oh my!" Gracie understood that Paul needed to be consoled. She searched her mind for words. The church had had lots of generous donors over the years, especially during its building campaign. Those bequests had been made before Paul had even come on board. But a scandal now was brewing, and sadly, too many people would take pleasure in the passing on of what too many others would be all too willing to believe.

"This is the first time I've ever been in this position," he told her sadly. "Mabel trusted me, so I talked to Nick Kendrick. Now, I wish I hadn't. I don't know what to do."

"Who else did you tell about this?"

He confirmed that he'd told only her, and Gracie tried to put it together in her own mind. "So, the inference is that you took advantage of a dying woman?"

"Mr. Kendrick reminded me that the Rohleder sisters were not 'on top of things.' Those were his words. I listened, and told him that we would honor Hazel's decision. And that I'd thought both women were very much on top of things. But now, as much as I'd like Eternal Hope to receive the bequest, I'd prefer the whole problem to go away.

Hazel certainly doesn't need the aggravation either."

Gracie assured Pastor Paul she was behind him one hundred percent. She hung up and said a quick prayer.

Lord, guide us, and protect the reputation of our pastor and our church. We love and honor him, and we trust him, and we are right to expect others to do the same.

Gracie toyed with her pocketbook, wondering if she'd been wrong to make this appointment to see Nick Kendrick on the pretext of discussing her own arrangements.

"It's difficult, confronting these issues," his secretary said, apparently sensing her discomfort. "But estate planning is a wise move. Mr. Kendrick's an expert."

"I'm sure he is." Gracie was determined not to prejudge this man who'd challenged the integrity of her pastor. She had no more than finished the sentence when the object of their exchange greeted her. The young attorney was wearing a light tweed jacket and a denim shirt. He had on pressed jeans and his dark brown hair showed wisps of gray.

"How nice to finally meet you," he said, holding out his hand. "I've heard a lot about you."

That surprised Gracie.

"From Kathleen Bailey. I've been going out with her." He gave a small smile.

That was an even bigger surprise. But at least he's not pulling his punches, Gracie thought and then wondered what a young woman she barely knew could have to say about her, but she decided not to pose that question. Nick Kendrick was probably just being polite.

He seated her in an overstuffed chair, then asked politely, "Can I offer you something? Coffee or tea?"

She just as politely declined and waited to let the Lord guide her next move.

How could she lie to this man? Carter had organized her papers, handled all the details of her estate. Gracie couldn't go through with the deception. She'd used reviewing her estate papers as an excuse for the appointment, but now she knew she had to come clean.

"I shouldn't be taking up your time."

Nick stopped her, his expression sympathetic. "Why don't we look at what you've brought? Many people are nervous about confronting the inevitable, but I assure you, it's a wise move. Your loved ones will be glad you took care of details."

He quickly looked over the papers in the portfolio Carter had created for her, as she explained that her niece was a lawyer in Chicago. "Carter insists that I bring my will up to date."

Closing the file, he handed it back to her. "Everything seems to be in order. Your niece did a thorough job." His gaze narrowed. "Now, what can I *really* do for you?"

Under his gaze, she felt herself stammering, trying to explain why she'd gotten involved. "I really came here to convince you that Paul Meyer is an honest and honorable man. Hazel Rohleder has convinced me that what he says is true: Her sister did intend that Eternal Hope benefit from her estate."

Nick leaned back in his chair, and put his index fingers to his lips, but still he made no comment.

Gracie felt hot, but there seemed no easy way to escape his scrutiny, so she rambled on, despite her better judgment. "Mabel wanted to give her money to Eternal Hope. Hazel is willing to vouch for her sister's wishes. I don't see where there's a problem."

Silence.

"I think we should honor Hazel's wishes," she now said more firmly. "I think you should give Hazel time to find that new will. Or respect her witness to what Mabel wanted done with her money."

He leaned forward. "First, let me say that I would be delighted actually to speak with Miss Rohleder. My secretary telephoned Hazel and her sister on several occasions to request an interview to go over the particulars of the estate. They promised to get back to her, but they never did.

"I was sorry to hear about Mabel's death, and sent my sincere condolences. My office dispatched to Miss Rohleder a copy of the terms of the life estate, and we asked her to have her lawyer contact us. To date I've had no response. She is leaving me with no choice but to request a court-appointed administrator, so that we can complete our obligations to the Horace Rohleder estate."

"She's an elderly woman, and she's grieving."

"I understand that, Mrs. Parks. That's why there has been to date no pressure from our office. We continue to handle her uncle's estate according to the terms provided in his will. But we also have a legal obligation to the state of Indiana, and the United States government, when one of the heirs to a life estate dies."

He was trying to be pleasant, but there was something about him. Why did she not trust the man?

"I'm sure Hazel intends to oblige, just give her time."

"Unfortunately, these things must be handled promptly."

Gracie promised to explain the urgency to Hazel.

"As for the situation with your pastor, he called me, asking for advice. I told him that I wasn't at liberty to give it, unless he had been appointed administrator for either sister, which he had not. He was making a claim, yet I had no corroborative information, and so I cautioned him.

"I pointed out that elderly people often feel indebted to caretakers and spiritual leaders. I advised him to be very careful in proceeding without legal documentation. This firm will honor the terms of the original will unless he has documentation warranting a change. He said he did not and was only inquiring on behalf of Hazel Rohleder. I told him that I did not think that it was wise to involve himself in her financial affairs."

The lawyer's smile now turned patronizing. "If he read something into that, then that is his problem. I'm simply doing my job."

Gracie had no reply.

"Really, Mrs. Parks, you can't imagine

how many times elderly clients call me, angry and feeling estranged, wanting to change their wills. I talk to them and the family, and things are usually worked out. They just don't want any problems, or to leave family members hurt and angry upon their deaths. They only desire to be loved and appreciated, but not everyone benefits from every decision."

"But Mabel and Hazel don't have family," Gracie pointed out.

He relaxed slightly. "I, for one, hope that is true. Yet a potential heir has contacted the firm. Whether or not there will be a claim on the estate is yet to be determined, but there has been an inquiry."

"Another heir? Does Hazel know?"

"A caller claiming to represent this heir contacted my office a few months back, but we require written documentation to release any information. As of yet, no one has made a formal request. If and when that happens, we will inform Miss Rohleder."

Gracie pondered the possibility.

"If Mabel Rohleder did die intestate — meaning without a will — then the court must appoint an administrator," he said.

"But you are the family lawyer."

"I took over the responsibility of managing the Rohleder estate when I became a partner in this firm. Several lawyers before me had handled it, and the executor is long deceased. But I am not the family lawyer. Both sisters made it clear that they did not want representation."

He met her gaze. "So, here we are discussing the intent of the life estate after the death of one of the heirs. The beneficiary, in this case, is the town of Willow Bend, which we also represent."

"Isn't that a conflict of interest?"

"Mrs. Parks," he began in a tight voice, "this is not a trial case, at least not yet. It's true, there is potential conflict of interest, but as of now, all parties have been satisfied with the terms. Should Hazel Rohleder produce a will naming her executor, I will be happy to work with her."

Gracie listened carefully, saying nothing. Hazel was depending on her. Even if she didn't know it.

Kendrick went on smoothly. "I assure you that the reputation of this firm is above reproach. The original partners were friends of Mr. Horace Rohleder. No one has any intention of challenging the provisions of his will. It is all very clear. The question remains as how best to serve Mr. Rohleder, his surviving heirs and Willow Bend."

"But do you have *Hazel's* best interest in mind?"

Nick Kendrick remained unreadable, his dark eyes unblinking as he measured her resolve. "None of us wants to face the possibility that we no longer can take care of ourselves."

"Hazel is *perfectly* capable," she challenged him.

"The death of one of the Rohleder heirs has made it necessary to evaluate the future of this estate. Hazel will be provided for, since the terms of the will are very clear. Now, if she would like to sit down and go over the particulars, I would be happy to do that with her."

"What if Mabel has a will? Would it make any difference?"

"I can't answer that until I see it. I don't mean to sound uncaring, Mrs. Parks, but I don't see what else we can do. Or you, for that matter. Unless, of course, you've turned up something else bearing on this matter."

No, she hadn't, but she was certainly going to try.

Opening the door of Abe's Deli, Gracie was pleasantly ambushed by the apple-and-cinnamon scented air, which was the best advertisement for her friend's daily bakery special. Gracie always loved the deli's welcoming atmosphere, yet today her appetite had deserted her. There was so much said, and too much unsaid, leaving her feeling unsettled and mistrustful of Nicholas J. Kendrick, attorney-at-law.

Rocky, already perched on a stool, beckoned her to join him. Abe Wasserman, the proprietor, appeared with a menu in hand, and curiosity in his friendly eyes. It was obvious Rocky had updated him on the current crisis.

"The pastrami is perfect. Lean, but not too lean," Rocky pronounced before taking another large bite of his sandwich.

As good as it smelled, the special of the day still didn't tempt Gracie, much to Abe's distress.

"What's this?" he demanded, pointing to the dish he'd placed in front of her on the counter. "You don't eat my potato kugel? You love my kugel! How about a bowl of chicken soup? It's my mother's recipe, with a little assist from Sophie, who knows a thing or two about seasoning."

"Just a hint of mint," Rocky reminded her. "Every time that sister of his arrives from Florida she tinkers with the already perfected formula."

Gracie glanced over the menu, and shook her head. "I've got too much on my mind."

Abe put the coffeepot on the counter, and looked her in the eyes. "You, Gracie Parks, worried? You think more of your problems than God's promises? Who's always reminding me of this, *huh?*"

"He's got a point." Rocky speared a forkful of potato salad.

She smiled. "You're right, Abe."

Abe put the plate in front of her again. "Of course, I am. Now, eat your kugel!"

Abe ladled out wisdom steeped in Jewish tradition as easily as he did his special chicken soup. Townsfolk, including herself, often came as much for the food for the soul served there as for the specialties of the house.

"Worry does no good, believe me," Abe said, filling her glass with water. "Most of the things I worried about never happened."

He grinned. "I left the worrying to my sister, she's got that market cornered."

"How *is* Sophie?" Gracie enjoyed his sister's visits. She usually breezed into town with a book full of new recipes and the determination to improve her brother's life.

"Sophie is Sophie. Her children are doing well, so now she has the grandchildren to worry about. The oldest just started pre-school and already she's worried about colleges."

Rocky looked at Gracie. "Sophie is Sophie. Stop the presses!"

"And Abe is Abe!" Gracie teased.

"I'll tell you what a smart lady once told me," Abe went on, ignoring them. "Why worry, she said, when you can pray? There wasn't a thing that she and God couldn't solve together, so where's the problem?"

"So what did Nick Kendrick say?" Rocky wanted to know.

Gracie confessed her failed attempt at deception, her embarrassment, and Nick's cool but reasonable-sounding response. "He makes sense, but at the same time he said a few things that concerned me. He's not above calling a competency hearing, I sensed that."

Abe furrowed his brow. "Who's this Nick Kendrick? Why doesn't he eat in my deli?"

"He's a young guy, Abe, so maybe he goes for tofu and bean sprouts at that natural food place out on the highway."

Abe dismissed the notion of such victuals with a wave of his hand. "You can't live on that stuff."

"You and I agree on that." Rocky took a bite of his bulging sandwich.

Gracie laughed. "Seriously, I don't know what to make of him. He seemed honest enough, but —"

"He's a politician," Rocky finished. "First and foremost. He doesn't have roots in Willow Bend, and I don't see him putting any down, either. His father's a lawyer and somehow connected to the partnership. I'd guess it's simply a parking place. If you're going to run for office, you've got to have somewhere to run from."

"Run from!" Abe echoed. "Sounds like Gracie's wishing he'd run away, pronto!"

Rocky shrugged. "I don't know what kind of politician he is — not yet, anyway. What I did find out is that he's good at his job, particularly in estate planning. He's very well respected. Kline and Paige have boasted about bringing him in as a partner, even at his age."

Gracie stared at Rocky.

"They don't call me Scoop Gravino for nothing," he told her modestly.

She gave a mock salute.

He laughed. "Okay, seriously. When you mentioned him managing the Rohleder estate the other night, I did a little detective work."

Abe refilled Rocky's coffee cup. "Everybody loves a mystery!" He sat down on his stool behind the counter. "So, this city slicker is here to run for office?"

"Kendrick comes from money, and he's got a political family. The Rohleder estate business could provide the leverage he needs to sell folks on his campaign."

Gracie pushed the kugel around with her fork. It didn't look good for Hazel. She would have to convince her to step forward and claim her right as administrator.

"I did discover something else today," Rocky broke into her gloom. "Horace Rohleder was married more than once. The first was annulled in Norfolk, Virginia, in 1943 by the parents of Olivia Martin Rohleder."

She stared at him. "But I knew that. Hazel mentioned it. I just wasn't paying attention."

"The wonder of computers. I looked it up in the newspaper archives, and *voilà!* I called the courthouse in Virginia, and in a matter of minutes, the clerk faxed me a copy of their marriage license."

"Was any other information given?"

"Miss Martin says she was eighteen, but my guess is that she was under the age of consent, or her parents could not have filed the annulment application."

"Was Horace in the military?" Abe wanted to know.

"Didn't check. Why?"

Abe stroked his chin. "We were at war. I knew a lot of impetuous young men who got themselves hitched right before shipping out, and Norfolk is a Navy base."

Could this be the background of the mysterious heir? The plot certainly was thickening!

7

Gracie surveyed the most recent changes Marge had made to her little gift shop. The window now displayed local crafts with a homespun flair. Her friend stocked an eclectic assortment of candles, greeting cards, novelty books, fashion accessories, plus unusual objects and handicrafts.

Her displays always showed off her talent for interior design, and this one featured a new collection of bright fabric wall hangings and quilts.

"Lovely!" Gracie told her. "Very colorful and inviting."

"Success!" Marge clapped her hands. "Now, what can I find by Willow Bend's own talented Comfort Harding? I usually have a selection of her work, but due to popular demand, I'm out right now. But, of course, you're looking for something *for* Comfort, not made by her."

"I want it to be practical, but thoughtful. Is that too tall an order?"

She picked up a bottle of bath soap and

unscrewed the top.

"*Hmm.* Apricot. Marge, can you get down that basket up there, please?"

Gracie busied herself collecting bath products, candles and a CD set of romantic classics while Marge retrieved a rag-weave basket from a high shelf. She scanned the rack for just the right card and found one for a wedding anniversary featuring a man and woman at a candlelit table. She laughed at another blank card bearing the likeness of a pumpkin-colored cartoon cat. "He looks like Gooseberry, don't you think?"

"We do have some get-well cards over there." Marge pointed to the other rack.

"I have a better idea. I'm going to write a gift certificate in each of these cards. One will be from Gooseberry to Lillian, inviting her to spend the night."

Gracie held up the anniversary card. "And in the other, I am going to put a menu, to be delivered for a romantic dinner for two. Love doesn't need an actual anniversary date to celebrate."

"Gracie Parks, you're brilliant! Let me sign the card, too. I'll help prepare the dinner, and the basket's on me."

"Deal!"

"I think I'll have Lillian help me with these when I pick her up at nursery school."

"Are you baby-sitting again?"

"No, I'm just going to take her home. Rick had an appointment this afternoon, so I volunteered. I have a care package from Abe to give them as well."

"Then let me include two big bows in the deal. Packages with pizzazz are all the more fun."

Gracie now examined a kit for making a ship in a bottle. "Just got that in. Maybe I was subconsciously recalling the one on your mantle." Marge smiled. "I remember El and Arlen had such fun putting it together."

"El loved the tall ships and the sea in general."

Marge came out from around the counter. "Why don't you buy this for Arlen for his birthday? I think I must have had him in mind. It could be from both of us."

Gracie hugged her friend. "You're the best!"

"I aim to please."

Marge handed her the basket. "And I'm a sucker for romance."

"Me, too," Gracie confessed.

"Now, Gracie," Marge said, switching subjects, "tell me the truth. What's going on with Hazel? I saw you talking to Pastor Paul, and I've heard the gossip."

Gracie sighed heavily as Marge told her what she'd already heard — basically the same story that Barb had told. It was beginning to look like a smear campaign against their pastor.

"The worst thing is that Jessica Larson has gotten in on the act. She's all gung-ho for that development at the edge of town, you know."

Gracie now filled Marge in on the Rohleder history, including the information about the earlier, annulled marriage.

"I was just a kid during the war years," Marge reminded her. "Honestly, Gracie, most people didn't know much about the Rohleders. We only were aware they were rich."

"It's curious. How this all will turn out is anyone's guess. But I can't resist a mystery, and this one's pretty baffling," said Gracie.

"There's one easy way to find out if Horace was in the military," Marge told her. "The cemetery. The VFW puts flags on all the veteran's graves, along with markers. The gravestones often give military information."

"I'd forgotten that."

"Why don't you wait until I close up, and I'll go with you. We'll stop at the nursery and pick up some flowers.

It was a matter of faith for Gracie that her beloved husband was not entombed in the Willow Bend cemetery, but happily enjoying his reward in heaven. Still, it would be nice to take fresh flowers to his grave. Chrysanthemums were in season, and El always loved autumn bronze and gold.

They made an itinerary. Gracie would stop in, as planned, to see the Hardings and Hazel, and they would later meet at the cemetery.

"Then we could go out for something to eat before choir practice," Marge suggested.

"Uncle Miltie has that chess tournament tonight. He's been looking forward to it for days. He loves to eat at the center with his pals, so this will give him the excuse. I'll give him a call on my cell phone."

"By the way," Marge said as Gracie was headed out the door, "a woman from the hospital auxiliary is going to call you about catering their annual Recognition Banquet."

Marge retrieved the woman's business card from behind the counter. "I told her that we could probably do it, but that I needed to check with you."

In fact, Gracie knew the dinner came at the same time every year. It was one of the regular jobs she looked forward to, since it honored the hospital volunteers, from the teenaged candy-stripers to the kindly ladies behind the counter of the gift shop. Such traditions dotted the Willow Bend calendar, and Gracie was proud of every one of them.

"See you in a little while!" she called back to Marge just as another customer passed her on the way in.

Comfort waved from the front porch when Gracie pulled into the Harding driveway with Lillian. It was hard to believe she'd undergone surgery so recently.

"Mommy!" Lillian tugged at the safety belt in the back seat to get herself undone.

Gracie got out to help her small passenger. She slipped the card certificates into the envelopes Lillian had decorated on the ride home from nursery school.

"You think you can carry this?" Gracie asked, after wedging the cards in the basket.

Lillian grinned, and happily took it in her arms after she got out of the back seat. "Thank you, Fannie Mae," she said courteously to Gracie's old blue Cadillac.

Gracie laughed.

"She's a great big car."

"*Shh*, she's a little bit sensitive about her size," Gracie teased. "Fannie Mae needs a larger than ordinary parking space and it embarrasses her."

Lillian put her finger to her lips and whispered, "Okay. But big is nice."

"So it is," Gracie agreed. "Did you hear that, Fannie Mae?"

Lillian giggled.

"I'm going to tell Mommy we need to give our car a name."

Gracie laughed. "You don't name a car, you listen. Yours will introduce herself."

Lillian bounded across the lawn carrying the basket.

Gracie grabbed Lillian's backpack and the goody box Abe had sent. She followed the mother and daughter into their house.

"This is so thoughtful!" Comfort held the cards for a long time, seeming to read them silently again and again.

She looked at Gracie with moist eyes. "I was leery of moving halfway across the United States, leaving everything and everybody I knew behind. I thought I was a city girl at heart and that I could never be happy in a little place like this. But Rick insisted I was going to love Willow Bend after he came here ahead of us. Gracie, you are so special — and please tell Marge how touched I am."

Lillian put her arms around her

mother's neck. "I helped."

Comfort admired the raggedy daisies decorating the envelopes and gave her daughter another squeeze.

"How are you feeling?" Gracie asked. "I must say, you look wonderful! I'd never guess that you'd just undergone emergency surgery."

"I'm a bit sore yet and will be, for a few weeks, anyway. I'm taking it slow, but I can do most of what needs done. Rick is a big help, too."

"I'm going to sleep with Gooseberry," Lillian told her mother. "He has his own bedroom."

Gracie laughed. "Actually, it's the guest room. He loves attention, and if you rub behind his ears and under his chin, he'll snuggle right down next to you, no questions asked."

"I know a little girl who needs a nap."

Lillian took the last bit of her snack and let Comfort gently touch a washcloth across her face. "You don't want to be tired and grumpy for Daddy. He's looking forward to your Old Maid game after supper tonight."

"I always win!" Lillian told Gracie proudly. "I can tell which card is the Old Maid — it's all bent and broken."

"Same telltale sign," Gracie said. "It's

116

nice to know that some things don't change. I'll have to play with little Elmo when I go visit him. I think I have his daddy's deck tucked away in a drawer somewhere."

Comfort chuckled. "That's another thing that doesn't change. I save everything of Lillian's, thinking of my someday grandbabies. Hair ribbons and wooden puzzle pieces, every sentimental souvenir!"

"It's memories we're trying to preserve," Gracie told her. "All those little treasures prompt them, and sometimes they're all we have left."

"I guess it's true that the best use of time is to spend it on something that will outlast us," Comfort said, reminding her of a sermon Pastor Paul had preached a couple weeks earlier. "You think God has His own memory chest? A box full of mementos of each of us, little nostalgic souvenirs of our great accomplishments for Him?"

"It is a beautiful thought, isn't it?"

"Sometimes Lillian and I sit and go through the things in the chest in our bedroom. She makes me tell her the story of each one, even though she's heard them a hundred times before."

Lillian now yawned.

"Well, I must get going." Gracie stood up. "I'm going to stop and visit Hazel."

Lillian scrambled to the refrigerator to pull off a drawing held up with colorful magnets. She handed Gracie a picture of a large house with what looked like several monuments in the yard, and female stick figures. One of them sported wings, and held what looked like a purple crayon.

"Please take this to Miss Hazel."

Gracie asked her to explain her picture and discovered the purple crayon was a chisel. Hazel, it seems, had finished all those sculptures for Mabel, who was now an invisible angel come to encourage her sister.

"She puts drawings on the refrigerator so Miss Mabel can see them in heaven," Comfort told her.

Gracie gave the child a big hug. "My husband used to say, 'We will enjoy heaven more if we keep a bit of it in our hearts while on earth.' Lillian's doing just that."

"She's learning from special saints. The ones at Eternal Hope — like you, Gracie. We went to a big church where we used to live. There were support groups for everyone and clubs of all types. Classes, too. The families with young children socialized with other families with small children. We never met people who weren't like us — busy couples just starting out in life!"

Comfort now slowly pushed herself to her

feet, holding her side and grimacing. "No position is comfortable for too long."

"Is there something else I can do? I love housework."

The younger woman laughed. "Don't tempt me, Gracie! I hate it! But really, we've had all kinds of offers of help. Marybeth insisted on coming over to clean this week. The Turner twins were here with enough casseroles to feed the whole church, and that's not to mention the half-dozen care packages that were delivered when I was in the hospital. Amy came over to see if I needed anything done. Even Estelle brought a pan of brownies. No, the Hardings are well provided for. And we love you all for it.

"You can do something for me, though," Comfort added, looking thoughtful. "Give Hazel a hug. She's having a hard day."

Gracie's mouth circled in surprise. "She seemed happy at the park yesterday."

"She's down in the dumps, and it's partly grief. That's natural. But she's frustrated at not being able to find that will. I know she doubts herself, and perhaps she's put undue emphasis on finding it, but I sure wish God would oblige her."

Gracie did, too.

"On top of everything, one of Mabel's fa-

119

vorite paintings was knocked down and damaged when Kathleen was dusting."

Gracie sighed. "Oh, dear!"

"Then she got a letter from the lawyer's office. They're petitioning the court to appoint an administrator. She needs a friend right now, Gracie. I just wish I felt better."

"Oh, Mommy!" Lillian rushed to embrace her mother.

"Give Hazel that hug! Don't forget!"

8

Gracie reached to touch the cold marble, and traced the engraved letters of her husband's name. She thought of the way she had loved to snuggle against him. Oh, he seemed so present! She could almost smell his Old Spice.

They'd planned to be grandparents, to retire and revel in the freedom it brought. They'd talked of traveling and buying a cabin on a lake. They'd shared a good life, it was true, but how she'd looked forward to sharing more years with him! She laid the flowers in front of the tombstone. "I miss you, El."

Gracie reread the words silently: *Elmo Parks; beloved husband and father.*

"I miss him, Marge."

Her friend stood by her side saying nothing, but speaking volumes. Arms intertwined, they leaned on each other.

They walked to the Rohleder site without talking. The pebbles on the path crunched underfoot. Horace Rohleder had indeed been a soldier. He'd served in France and Germany during World War I.

Gracie and Marge stood in front of his grave. He had wanted to provide for his cherished nieces and the town he loved. How could he have known what problems his legacy would cause?

"Maybe Abe was right, and Horace fell in love while waiting to be shipped off to war."

Gracie's gaze was on the new grave nearby. Did Mabel know something Hazel didn't? What caused her agitation that day she'd sent for Paul? Why such a baffling bequest? If only Mabel could tell them!

But she can't, Lord. How will we know her intentions? And how do we protect her sister?

Kathleen was washing the windows on the front porch when Gracie and Marge arrived at the Rohleder house. "Hazel's in her studio working," the young woman told them.

"Oh, how wonderful!" Marge exclaimed. "God heard our prayers."

Kathleen informed them, "I'm not religious."

"Neither am I," Gracie said in all honesty. "Sometimes religion gets in the way of a friendship with God."

"I'm not sure I even believe in God."

Kathleen dropped her rag in the bucket forcefully enough to punctuate that remark.

Gracie was not intimidated. "God believes in *you,* dear."

"Why should He?" Kathleen spun around to face Gracie. "People have this idea that there's some benevolent, omnipotent being who cares for humanity. Me, I'm not convinced. Nothing I've experienced reinforces that idea. If God's anything, He's ambivalent at best."

Gracie glanced at Marge, who seemed equally lost for words. In the silent communication that passed between them they prayed for Kathleen.

You know her heart, Lord. Help us to see her as You do.

"There's much I don't know about God." Marge stepped forward. "But what I do know about Him has changed my life."

Kathleen hugged herself.

"He cares for me," Marge told her. "He loves all of us. God listens to our prayers and answers. I know He intends our difficulties in life not to break us, but to make us stronger. We draw that strength from Him."

Kathleen met her gaze. "That's all well and good for you."

Gracie's heart went out to this desperate

123

young woman. There was something breaking inside of Kathleen, and the damage was spreading.

"There are no qualifications for God's love," Gracie explained. "He gives grace freely. We're the ones who insist on putting limits on Him."

Kathleen struggled to maintain composure, but Gracie could see tears just below her stony facade.

Gracie quietly lifted the young woman to God.

"I'm sorry," Kathleen said unexpectedly, with her back to them as she stooped to gather the cleaning supplies. "I spoke out of turn. I didn't mean to sound so disrespectful."

Marge took a step in friendship, reaching out to touch her shoulder, but the young woman kept her focus on her task.

"I broke up with my boyfriend last night," Kathleen said, even more unexpectedly.

"Oh, dear," Marge whispered. "I'm so very sorry."

Gracie wondered if she meant Nick Kendrick, but decided it was not the best time to ask.

Kathleen stood up and turned around, brushing away the tears. "It's not like it was serious or anything. He was just a guy — a self-centered guy. I hate him."

"Broken hearts mend, but they ache terribly in the process. We're praying for you, my dear," Gracie said.

"If you'll excuse me, I have work to finish." Kathleen straightened her shoulders and bent to grab the bucket.

Lord, I don't know what to do to help this poor sad child, but it's clear she's in need of Your love — and yet I don't know the best way to reach her. Guide me, please.

Hazel herself was much cheerier than Gracie expected, given Comfort's earlier report. Marge and Gracie followed her to the airy studio. Its windows, like those on the sun porch, were curtainless, and pots of assorted ferns vied for the last rays of the day's sunshine.

Stacks of magazines and newspapers, racks of canvases, assorted toolboxes, and baskets of rocks in various shades of gray, pink and sandstone littered the room. On a bench sat a large gilt frame that held a charcoal portrait of the two middle-aged sisters, its glass broken. Gracie deduced that that was the damaged treasure, and walked over to take a better look.

"Can it be repaired?" Marge wanted to know.

It was Hazel who broke the silence. "The tear was an accident, but maybe it was meant to be. Seeing it jarred me, shocked me maybe more than the nurse's report that Mabel was really dead."

She sighed. "In a strange way, maybe this accident had to happen. It was the destruction of that portrait that compelled me to go to work. I was so upset, nothing else would distract me."

Hazel turned to face the worktable in the center of the room, where there was a sculpture in process. An air chisel and protective glasses lay nearby. Gracie and Marge walked over to admire the piece.

They studied the large chiseled hunk of rock. It was more angular than the others; much too modern for Gracie's taste, but, like the sculptures on the sun porch, the interplay of shadow and light on its curves had a pleasing effect.

"So, what do you think?" Hazel asked.

"It's . . . lovely," Marge blurted.

Gracie studied the piece, wishing she had a more nuanced appreciation of art. She ran her hand along the arch. "It's very different from your other pieces. A stronger statement, I think."

"You're becoming an art critic!" Hazel's tone was lighthearted. "Marble is a harder stone. And I'm in a harder place.

"I don't understand modern art," Marge confessed. "But I like this piece. It's more geometric than the others, it's true, but it's not hard at all."

Hazel took a step backwards. "That's the wonder of art. You don't have to understand it to appreciate it. And even if you don't appreciate it, or are repelled by it, good art speaks to you, just the same. It doesn't back down, or even compromise."

She pushed herself up on her stool. "I don't know what this piece is saying yet. I've never created anything without Mabel nearby."

"I guess you'll just have to listen to it," Marge told her.

"I haven't sculpted since Mabel took sick. I am an old woman, and there are so many young new artists. I have arthritis in my fingers and joints. Perhaps it's crazy to think I still can create something of enduring value."

She laced her fingers and, grabbing one knee in her cupped hands, seemed to study her work. "I don't know why I'm creating this, except I can't *not*. It's good to be working again. Perhaps it's my last chance to create the piece I want to live after me. I want to be remembered, like every other artist. I'm satisfied with most of my creations, but I long to create the one I think is still inside me."

Gracie recalled the discussion she'd just had with Comfort about memorabilia and treasures of the heart. Comfort was collecting things to outlive her in memory. Gracie's hope chest held mementos of motherhood, and blessed reminders of the life she'd shared with her beloved El. But she'd also saved thank-you notes, cards and letters of gratitude from friends she'd touched along the way.

But, of course, these friends had touched her, too.

It dawned on Gracie that although she was not an artist, she, too, had created an important work. Hadn't she raised a child to be a good father and husband? *You opened doors for me, Lord, and they led to avenues of love and grace. We all create through You.*

"There was something you said about not knowing why you're doing this." Gracie looked at Hazel. "It just struck me, that's what you need — to *know* why. Allow God to speak to your heart, and He will."

She was excited about where her thoughts were leading, and could hardly find words quickly enough. "Perhaps it's time to ask God to reveal what He wants you to see."

Hazel smiled at her.

"For me, it's usually the fear of failing that gets me waylaid," Marge broke in. "I start to think, 'Who am *I* to do this?' "

Gracie had often been in the same predicament. "Yes, I know the feeling. But I pray, and the voice inside of me says, 'Who are you *not* to do that?' "

"It is often a matter of will," Hazel agreed, "even for the artist."

The older woman seemed to be considering Gracie's words. "Not my will," Hazel said, softly, "but Thy will be done."

Gracie and Marge both smiled in agreement.

"It's always been hard for me to pray," Hazel conceded. "I used to pray with Mabel, but it was her faith carrying us. That's being honest. Now that she's taken that faith with her, the truth is, I seem to be lost."

They stood quietly for a long moment, Gracie silently imploring the Lord for guidance. She'd discovered that an important part of praying is a willingness to be part of the solution.

"But how can God's will be so cruel?" Hazel asked a little desperately. "I wanted us to go together. We did everything together." She forced a smile in spite of her tears. "I used to joke that if one of us had to go first, it should be me. Mabel's faith would carry her. After all, it had always been strong enough for both of us."

Marge regarded Hazel with kindness. "That's what friends are for — to carry you to the Lord when you're not able to go on your own."

There were no miracles without that openness to participation. That truth had been borne out for Gracie over a lifetime of experience.

"You both are pointing the way," Hazel told them. "I can see that now."

Kathleen appeared at the door with a tea tray, but did not enter. "I thought you'd like a break."

"How thoughtful of you. We'll take it on the patio."

Kathleen busied herself with pouring and offering cookies, resisting Hazel's coaxing her to join them. Gracie feared that she and Marge were the reason for the girl's reluctance.

Lord, help me to talk to Kathleen. Let there be no miscommunication between us. Let her hear, as You would have her understand.

"I probably won't be home until after you're in bed," Kathleen informed Hazel. "I'm going out with some friends after class."

"Another date with that young man who calls here once in a while?"

Kathleen looked past Hazel. "It didn't work out."

Kathleen had been going out with Nick Kendrick, yet she had never mentioned his name to Hazel. Gracie couldn't help but wonder what this meant. Was it merely self-protective shyness . . . or something more sinister?

"Where are you from, Kathleen?" Gracie decided to ask.

"Nowhere, really."

Gracie found this answer odd. "Nowhere?"

"Well, Avery, most recently. I've moved around a lot. When I got this job and Hazel offered room and board, it made financial sense to stay here."

Kathleen gave a little smile, but it was hard to tell what she was thinking. When she spoke again, she said, "Maybe while I'm gone, you could return those calls. I put the list and numbers by the phone, along with the mail that needs to be gone through." The young woman's expression now was kind. "I wish I could do it for you, but I can't."

Hazel didn't reply.

"Please," Kathleen pleaded. "When you

131

don't return the calls, it makes it look like I don't give the messages to you."

Hazel glanced toward the garden. "Winter will be here before we know it. We should probably cover those rose bushes. Mabel always did."

Gracie impulsively reached for Hazel's hand. She lifted her eyes heavenward. "Lord, we're about to embark on a painful journey. We have to examine the treasures and souvenirs of a life well lived, and decide what to keep and what to give away. Give us strength, and peace in knowing that Mabel is with You now, and gives us her blessing to do what we must."

They sat in silence for a moment. "Gracie and I have time to help you go through Mabel's things," Marge told Hazel. "Sorrow is easier when it's divided up. And that's what friends are for, remember?"

Hazel agreed to discuss plans, and this caused Kathleen to seem genuinely relieved. Gracie suspected that the cold angry aura she presented to the world was the smallest, least definitive part of this troubled young woman.

How to help her be whole again, that was the challenge.

9

Pastor Paul was still in his office when Gracie arrived for choir practice, so she decided to drop in for a moment. His desk was laden with thick volumes of Biblical commentary, and he was seated at his computer.

She apologized for disturbing him, but was secretly glad he was there. Her time with Kathleen and Hazel lay heavily on her mind.

"I needed a break." Paul put his hands behind his head.

"You're sweet to say that, but I suspect mine is just one of the many interruptions you've had today."

"Actually, I wouldn't say I'm all that popular." He laughed. "Folks usually don't just pop in on the pastor — present company excluded."

He flashed a grin. "As you know, I do like to be here in the early evening. Most nights something's going on, and I amble out to make an appearance. That's when folks talk to me, or ask for an appointment if they need special time. I'm glad you stopped by, Gracie."

Gracie told him how Comfort was doing, and he gave her the schedule of people providing meals for them for the next week. They also discussed the upcoming birthday party, and Barb Jennings's offer to head up the affair.

"Barb and the Rohleders have enjoyed a special friendship since she was a girl. She'd love to do it, she says."

"I just learned about their relationship," Paul told her. "Reminding me once again to never take for granted that I know my flock. Such surprises delight me, the way people connect at different stages of their lives."

"Barb's excited about the musical program we're working on," Gracie told him.

"It will be a wonderful event, I'm sure of it." He smiled at her.

Paul leaned back in his chair now, his expression more serious. "You're probably wondering what's the latest with the Rohleder estate."

He told her Nick Kendrick had called him, to say that he was filing a motion requesting Hazel be evaluated by a court-designated psychologist. He was asking to be appointed administrator of Mabel's estate. "He said he was letting me know so I could give Hazel guidance. She never has called him back to respond to any of his previous requests for information.

"You know, he actually seems to have Hazel's best interests at heart. It's a difficult situation for all concerned."

Gracie replied, "We're going to go through Mabel's belongings tomorrow. Maybe we'll turn up the will, in the nick of time."

"The court wants things to be handled in a timely manner. Hazel has avoided the inevitable. Kendrick does have the fact of her evasion on his side. She just won't deal with it.

"I told him to pray about it. He needs to be at peace with his decision. If he prays, and still is convinced Hazel cannot manage her financial affairs, then he's obligated to go forward with the petition. He seemed receptive to that."

How could anyone not respect such an honorable man as Paul Meyer? There *had* to be a will, she was just sure of it. Finding it would settle things once and for all.

"I've talked this matter over with the trustees," Paul told her. "We all agreed to handle the rumors by pointing out that Eternal Hope will honor the court settlement of the estate."

He leaned forward. "Gracie, you know how much I love Willow Bend, and this congregation. I've prayed about it, and I'm at peace with our decision. If all the money goes to the town, so be it. Everything belongs to God anyway, and it's fitting we've trusted the outcome to Him."

Gracie respected his position, but feared what it might wind up costing the only Rohleder heir to keep everyone happy. What if settling the estate meant Hazel had to give up living on her own?

"Our generation has a tendency to dismiss the value of aging, and the wisdom that comes with it," he told her. "After retiring, my parents embraced a second career of mission, and I'm just finally coming to appreciate the real value of that choice."

"*Over* the hill is not *under* it, as my sage old uncle is fond of saying. We've all got a lot of splendid years left in us. Hazel Rohleder included."

He chuckled. "I've been thinking a lot about how to bring the experience of our seniors together with the energy and enthusiasm of the youth of our church."

"You've done that with prayer partnering. It's already a wonderful success. The relationship between Lillian and Hazel is a perfect example."

He nodded thoughtfully. "Yes, but we can do even more. We have to hear more of the stories, the faith journeys of our church family members. We must listen to each other more."

She loved this young shepherd and was proud to be one of his flock.

"Thanks for getting involved, Gracie. Both for Hazel's sake and my own."

"Thank you, Paul."

"On another note, and in answer to prayer, the board decided that regardless of the estate gift, Eternal Hope is going to establish a memorial fund in honor of both of the sisters."

"That's wonderful to hear."

Estelle seemed in a much better mood this choir practice. She was even helping Barb plan her musical celebration of the Rohleders.

Marybeth handed Gracie the folder of music for the program. "Herb says that Hazel's lawyer called him, asking questions about Hazel."

"What did he say?"

Marybeth looked uneasy. "He had to be honest. She's had a half-dozen citations in the last year — parking violations mostly. Pray for him, Gracie. The lawyer implied he might be asked to sign a statement. Herb hates being put in this position, having to provide information that could be misconstrued."

"He can only be honest." Gracie would trust God.

Marybeth sighed and gave Gracie a fast hug.

Marge was waiting her turn to talk to Gracie and pulled her aside. "Jeffrey stopped at the store. He's got my inventory entered and a program set up that works with the new computerized cash register! Bless his obnoxious little heart!"

"Are you having trouble with him?" Gracie knew Jeffrey Larson could be a handful.

"I like him, really. I was just teasing. Once you get past the big show of attitude, you realize he's very insecure. I tell you, Charlotte likes him, too, and dogs have a good sense of people."

"Cats, as well."

Marge laughed. "Jeffrey told me that his mother is going to work for Nick Kendrick's campaign. Frankly, I suspect Jessica's the one behind the rumors. I hear she's coming to the fellowship committee meeting."

Yes, Lord, we are going to need Your guidance — plus a whole lot of good will.

138

★ ★ ★

Rocky and Uncle Miltie were engaged in the final moves of their checkers match when Gracie returned from choir practice. She kissed her uncle, then got an update on his evening, including positive raves for the chicken-fried steak dinner at the senior center.

"Arlen called," Rocky reminded him.

"Oh, yeah, and I heard all of little El's latest knock-knock jokes."

Gracie went to telephone her only child and his family. Arlen and Wendy had been to the theater to see a ballet in which one of Wendy's students starred. As she listened to them in turn, Gracie thanked God for answering another prayer.

Arlen had been uncertain about his wife's returning to work before Elmo was in school full time. For her part, Wendy had longed to be teaching dance again yet felt compromised by a part-time schedule. So, renting a studio in their own building, she began to build a career on her very doorstep.

Of course, Gracie secretly wished her loved ones would give up the big city and move to Willow Bend where she could regularly spoil her only grandchild.

"Hi, Gramma!" It was the sweet voice of her grandson.

Rocky came in carrying empty glasses. "*Ah*, it's Elmo! I can tell by your expression." When she finally hung up, he was leaning in the doorway. "I hear they've got some real airfare bargains to La Guardia."

"It's hard to be so far away, especially when he's this young. I won't recognize him in a couple of months."

He pooh-poohed that notion. "Of course you'll know him. He looks just like his granddad."

They were a happy family, and Gracie knew she had much to be thankful for. *Lord, forgive me for ever feeling sorry for myself.*

She looked fondly at Rocky for a moment. Recalling the words from the Psalm, she whispered, "Delight yourself in the Lord; And He will give you the desires of your heart."

"Amen," he proclaimed, "but what if I desire some fudge-chunk cookies?"

"Just follow me."

"Did I hear the words 'fudge-chunk'?" Uncle Miltie called out. "I've got my cookie radar on."

"I talked to Nick Kendrick today," Rocky told them, happily wiping the crumbs off his trousers. "Can I, pretty please, have another one?"

"I hope you had more success with the

man than I did. I felt like such a fool."
Gracie passed him the cookie tin.

"I called him to confirm the quotes for a story we're running on the proposed extension of the sewage system for property beyond the edge of town. It just so happens that he's the new owner of some of that property."

Uncle Miltie scowled. "A small conflict of interest, I'd say."

"I brought that up to him — as a candidate for state assembly, he *should* see the conflict but doesn't seem to. It's an investment, he claims, and if he can make something happen for Willow Bend, it's his belief everyone benefits.

"Things seem to be leading in the direction of some trouble over that land. We're just far enough from Chicago to appeal to a new generation who work out of home offices. Computers, the Internet and cell phones have changed the way folks do business.

"Willow Bend doesn't have the commercial appeal of Avery, but a fancy new housing development could change that. Kendrick implied as much. So look for an upcoming fight."

"Well, we don't want his changes!" Uncle Miltie's face was getting red. "We've voted down proposals to commercialize Willow Bend before. Who is he to come in here and try to railroad through his plan?"

Rocky shrugged. "They're not just his ideas. What I'm saying is a fact of life, whether we like it or not. People are moving out into the country. These newcomers have some dough and expect bigger and more luxurious homes. And services to match."

"But part of Willow Bend's charm is its . . . charm," Gracie said.

"We can keep that by not bringing in every chain store on the planet and subdivisions full of McMansions!" Uncle Miltie was practically shouting by now.

"Calm down," Rocky soothed him.

Gracie remembered the young women in the park. "I'm counting on compromise. That's why we have a town meeting and elect a council."

She could only hope — and pray — that what she said was true. She loved having new families settle down in Willow Bend, and recognized how important cultural opportunities, shopping and entertainment had become to this younger generation that had more money to spend — or maybe just more credit cards.

"What do you think Nick Kendrick plans

to do with the Rohleder estate funds?" she ventured.

"Old Horace wanted it donated to the cultural enrichment of the community he loved."

"That sounds like a quote," Uncle Miltie's tone was still on the surly side. "Don't tell me Kendrick's going to use it in his campaign."

"Tom Ritter reminded the town council that we've always had progressive citizens like Horace Rohleder," Rocky said.

"But they can't do anything with that money while Hazel is still alive. Don't they realize that?"

Rocky dunked his cookie. "That's where you're wrong. I was talking about the story with Ann O'Neill, the lawyer who's on our side of the development issue. She says all Kendrick has to do is petition for the court to appoint a legal guardian for Hazel. And as long as there's enough money from the estate held for her care, the administrator could access the rest.

"She told me that there is actually a formula for calculating things like that based on life expectancy charts."

"Which Hazel has surpassed," Uncle Miltie pointed out. "Yours truly, George Morgan, has also topped those charts. So

143

how do they account for *that, hmm?*"

"They don't have to. The formula does factor longer longevity in the calculations. The administrator need only provide for maximum longevity and a standard of living comparable to the terms of the life estate. Believe me, they're used to working these things out!"

Gracie shook her head. "Oh my!"

"Why should the town have to wait to access the money?" said Rocky. "Here's a big project ready to go, and Nick Kendrick stands ready to push it. That's going to be his case. He'll argue that it's an important window of opportunity. If not Willow Bend, then one of the nearby towns will profit from the growth. Willow Bend has no monopoly on available land."

Uncle Miltie pounded the table. "Whose side are you on, man?"

"I'm not taking sides. I'm just telling you like it is." Rocky glared at her uncle. "Change is in the wind, old buddy, like it or not. It's just a matter of time."

"Then I hope I'm not around to see it!" Uncle Miltie snapped.

"What harm lies in developing that piece of land? If we do it now, while we old-timers still have a strong voice in the council, we can probably limit the damage. It seems inevitable it will be developed, so why not make our desires known? We can do this sensibly and, as Gracie said, by compromising."

"I'm all for progress." Uncle Miltie agreed. "But when progress means I don't recognize my town any more, then I like things the way they used to be."

Rocky nodded. "I don't blame you, but we've got to be pragmatic. We need a vision of our own for the future, if they're going to listen to us. That's what I was talking to Ann about. I think this estate thing can be settled to the benefit of all concerned."

Gracie nodded. "I guess I'm sometimes afraid of the future, too. I wonder what Willow Bend will look like in twenty years. What are to be the consequences of the decisions we make now?"

"The reality is, we have no control over the tide, Gracie. We can ride it, even harness it for our benefit, but we can't stop it. I say we work to use it to secure a way of life we can proudly pass down to future generations."

"Unfortunately, to some people, Hazel Rohleder seemed to stand smack in the way of progress. Rocky, as I see it, there's only one way Willow Bend is going to get fast access to that money."

She met Rocky's gaze. "By declaring Hazel incapable of handling her own affairs." If the surviving sister was judged incompetent, she'd be forced to give up her house and go to a nursing home. Mabel's death had been hard on Hazel, but this would surely kill her.

"We can't let that happen," Rocky agreed. "Even if most folks see her as eccentric or reclusive, Hazel's part of the fabric of this town. She ought to be able to control her own destiny as long as she is physically able."

"Don't forget there's also the matter of Mabel's own intent for her estate," Uncle Miltie reminded them. "Some unpleasant things have been said about our pastor, and I think a priority is to get his name cleared."

"Right now, I have to say I think anything the church does will just compound the problem," Rocky said. "It's probably better to concentrate on Hazel — and meanwhile pray that that will is found."

Gracie suddenly had an inspiration. "What do you think about sponsoring an art show?"

"Huh?"

"The paper, I mean."

She pressed on. "You love getting out your tools, right? Why don't you fix up that

146

unused first-floor storeroom you've got? Use it for rotating art exhibits? People would drop into the *Gazette* office to see them, after reading your features on local artists."

"Why do I suppose you have an artist in mind?"

"Because you know me so well, that's why."

10

Gracie took Marge along with her when she went to pitch her idea to Hazel the next day. Kathleen had already left for class, and at the dining room table, Hazel was up to her elbows in paper clutter.

"Kathleen and I have boxed up most of Mabel's clothing, but there's still a lot to tackle. Pastor Paul offered to come by and pick up everything for the next rummage sale when we're done. I told him I'd call him when we were ready."

She smiled at Gracie and Marge. "Thanks for agreeing to pitch in."

They followed Hazel to the music room, which had become a converted bedroom for Mabel during those last months when she couldn't get up and down the stairs.

Hazel told them, "After supper, Kathleen and I tackled Mabel's closet. She was so patient, encouraging me to ramble on about my sister, and our life in this house."

Hazel paused in front of the now emptied closet. "Everything smelled of Mabel's lilac perfume, and it became too much for me. I broke down, and Kathleen put her arms around me.

"Then, out of nowhere, she asked about the hat I'd hung on the bedpost to give to Lillian. It was the most innocent question," Hazel explained. "But it brought back memories of my sister and my aunt, in their white gloves and stylish hats."

She looked at them. "My aunt adored pretty things, and so did Mabel. I, on the other hand, liked plainer, more sensible clothes, more like young women wear now — practical for work and play."

Hazel went on, her expression confiding. "I was secretly happy when hats and gloves went out of style. My sister, however, stubbornly clung to her favorites, in the hopes they'd come back into vogue."

Hazel looked around her and sighed. "You're right, this is a difficult task."

Gracie reminded her, "You don't have to get rid of it all now. We can put some of it away for you."

A smile lit up Hazel's eyes. "No, I'm certain Mabel would rather I not move backward. We gave away so much while she was living, she wouldn't want me hoarding things for grief's sake."

Hazel looked at Gracie. "I now see mem-

149

ories as glorious intruders, sweet salve whenever they barge into our consciousness. Nostalgia longs for the place we can never return — I understand that now."

Marge's eyes were wet, and Gracie's too.

After retrieving from the car the empty cartons they'd picked up at the Willow Mart, Gracie and Marge packed clothing. Kathleen had removed all the clothing from the dresser and stacked it in piles on the bed. Hazel now went through her sister's jewelry, keeping out special pieces to give as gifts.

"Are you okay?" Marge wanted to know.

Gracie nodded. "Thankful. That's what I am."

"Friends are our chosen families," Marge said with feeling.

Gracie mentioned that Pastor Paul was bringing over a couple of teenagers to carry the boxes. "We'll call him when we finish."

"Ask him to make Jeffrey one of the ones he calls. He needs to get away from his computer screen."

Hazel appeared beside them holding a gold filigree leaf brooch and a beautiful silver watch. "You choose. Mabel would want you each to have something to remember her by."

Gracie accepted the brooch, hugging

Hazel. Marge took the watch, slipping it on her wrist and holding it up to admire it. *"Oooh!"* She said. "It's gorgeous."

Then she, too, hugged Hazel. "What was I saying about putting sentimentality aside and getting back to work?" Marge teased her.

"You have your job cut out for you! We've still got a lifetime collection of papers here to sort."

"You've probably already thought of it," Gracie now said, "but I was wondering if Mabel had a special box where she kept her valuables?"

"There's actually a safe, but we never used it. I don't even know the combination."

Gracie was intrigued. "Don't you think we should look?"

"It was cleaned out after Uncle Horace's death, and we never bothered with it."

"El and I had a safety-deposit box at the bank," Gracie told Hazel. But then Gracie remembered that law required the box be sealed upon the death of one of the depositors, unless the survivor was the husband or wife. The bank would have contacted Hazel, and, besides, it seemed unlikely Mabel would have kept such a thing secret from her sister.

Marge couldn't resist asking, "Where do you keep all your important documents and family papers?"

"In drawers, behind picture frames, tucked in vases. It depends on what it is. Mabel kept her passport in a sachet bag inside her lingerie drawer with her birth certificate and Social Security card."

"And you? Where do you keep your own documents?"

"I keep any important papers in the roll-top desk in the study."

"I'm sure you've already checked Mabel's drawer, haven't you?"

"It was the first place I checked. I even looked in the little room she had upstairs, although she hadn't used it for more than a year." She looked at Marge and Gracie. "I'm forgetful, but not completely senile — not yet anyway."

"We're all forgetful," Gracie noted ruefully.

"Still, one needs to retain a sense of humor about losing one's mind. Your taking such care with my feelings is definitely appreciated, believe me. But I do wonder how long I will be able to take care of myself."

"From what you've told me about Mabel, she seems to have been so orderly, organized." It seemed to Gracie that Mabel had known what she was doing and somehow left a clue as to the whereabouts of her will. "She didn't have any other special box or secret place?"

"We didn't bother so much about documents — we never found them much fun, if you want to know the truth. Small-minded things! I think we tried to pretend they didn't exist — I guess we were just a pair of bohemians at heart!"

Hazel looked thoughtfully at Gracie. "You were right to send me to the Lord in prayer. I was holding Him responsible for letting my sister slip away. Mabel never once doubted His care. But me . . . well, I've always wanted things my own way."

Marge answered her just as thoughtfully. "We all get caught up in our pain, alienating ourselves from the true source of comfort. Each one of us has expectations of God."

"His ways are always the best," Gracie said softly.

"I think I simply had to realize how unbearable it is to be without God," Hazel explained. "Wherever I was, Mabel was always somewhere nearby. When I was working on my own, I could still feel her presence, or hear her playing the piano. I

guess I thought I didn't need anyone else —
not even God."

The three of them sat in silence for a few
minutes, basking in sympathetic compan-
ionship and God's love.

"It's time for tea," Hazel announced with
a warm smile. "I feel so much better I even
have an appetite, all of a sudden!"

They bustled about the kitchen together
gathering what they needed in order to have
tea on the sun porch. Hazel was humming
to herself as she got down a special set of
earthenware plates from a high shelf. As she
watched her, Gracie smiled: Nick Kendrick
would have a hard time proving his case.

Hazel looked out the porch window.
"We'd often wake up at the crack of dawn,
and Mabel would bring us tea out here.
We'd eat our breakfast on the patio when
the weather was nice."

"It's a lovely place — a kind of oasis in
your own house."

Hazel nodded gratefully. "That's exactly
how I feel, Gracie."

They sipped quietly. As she sat there,
Gracie mentioned her idea of the art show,
and Rocky's willingness to sponsor it.
"You're the perfect local artist to inaugurate
the space! Please say you'll agree!"

"Well, I can hardly say no," Hazel told

her. "What kind of Willow Bender would I be if this chance to share my work with my community made me feel less than very, very proud?"

Gracie's eyes sparkled. "We're proud, too — proud to have you here!"

"I only wish Mabel could enjoy the opening and all the preparations with me!" Hazel's tone was low, though her expression was serene.

Later, while they sorted papers, Marge took a deep breath and said, "You really do need a lawyer."

"I don't want Nick Kendrick!" Hazel was adamant.

"You said Mabel was distraught the day she asked you to call Pastor Paul," Gracie quickly changed the subject. "But that was out of character, in light of what you have just told us. Something, or someone, provoked her."

"I thought at the time it was her medication," Hazel explained. "But it could have been a combination of pain and her failing sense of control over her life. But you're right. That day it seemed to come out of nowhere. We were talking about art — my sculpture, to be exact. I'd received that letter from the gallery in Chicago. And she was trying to talk me into doing the piece."

155

Marge picked up a paper from the top of a pile. "This one."

Hazel nodded. "Mabel was still having some good days. She'd been up and around, nagging me to get started. That's when the subject of wills came up. Mabel seemed to think my work was valuable. She insisted that I write a will. In my usual fashion, I chided her for not practicing what she preached. She got defensive, saying that she had, in fact, written one. I tried to make light of it, wanting to change the subject — but she kept coming back to it. I thought I could joke it away. The more I avoided it, the more she pushed. I know it was foolish, but I just couldn't face the idea of her mortality, or my own, for that matter."

Gracie understood the aversion. She'd balked when El insisted they see a lawyer to update their arrangements and to make out living wills. She knew it was the practical thing to do. She and El would thus spare their only child agonizing decisions, but she hadn't wanted to deal with it either.

"So you didn't do anything about it?" Marge asked Hazel. "Well, you're going to do something about it now, even if I have to take you to a lawyer's office myself."

"Yes, my dear," Hazel said meekly. "I know you're right."

156

Gracie remained convinced there was a will in the house. She urged Hazel to tell them more about that day.

"Mabel's insistence on talking about her will made me upset, I couldn't help it. So I left her with Kathleen and ran some errands. When I came home, she was delirious, not making sense at all. She was rambling about the past.

"Kathleen said the hospice nurse had been there, and so I attributed her irrationality to the medication."

Gracie was making mental notes.

"She asked to see Pastor Paul the next day. She was quite sharp, then. But she wouldn't tell me anything. And by the time he got there, the medication again had taken effect, and she kept slipping in and out of consciousness, confusing the present with the past. It was hard on Paul. We both realized the end was near.

"He prayed with me, and she came to her senses again, just like that. That's when she told him she wanted money to go to the church. Mabel made me promise that I would follow her instructions and ensure they honored her bequest.

"What exactly that bequest was, she didn't say. Soon she was, unfortunately, not making any sense at all."

157

"You never saw her write that will."

Hazel shook her head.

"She loved the church family at Eternal Hope, and felt enormous affection for Pastor Paul. Gratitude, too. Like I said, both Mabel and I considered Lillian a ray of sunlight, our own personal merry angel. Sending her here had been his idea. Mabel wanted to do something to show how much it had meant to her. We talked about that. She said that she would write it all down for me."

"But she died before she had a chance to do that," Marge finished for her.

Gracie thought of Kathleen. What did they know of this young woman? Could she in some way be involved with the missing document?

"Was Kathleen present at the time? She could have acted as a witness," Gracie asked now.

"No, she wasn't."

She'd been dating Nick Kendrick, however. He'd said so himself. Gracie wasn't sure how to broach the subject.

"If it's up to me, Eternal Hope will receive the bulk of Mabel's estate. That seems to be what she wanted." Hazel was thinking aloud.

"Ann!" Marge exclaimed. "Ann O'Neill!

She's the lawyer to get. She's a good lawyer and a loyal friend. Everyone loves and respects her."

"And she has no political aspirations," Gracie added.

Marge's tone was firm. "Hazel, the longer you wait, the harder it's going to be to convince the court that you are the best administrator."

"That means I have to steel myself to approach Nick Kendrick, you know it does."

"I'm afraid so."

Gracie glanced at Marge, not at all convinced that Hazel Rohleder was up to confronting the young lawyer alone. It was like the lamb confronting the wolf without her shepherd.

"Why don't you talk to Ann before you see him?"

"I'll do what you say, Gracie. I know you have my best interests at heart."

11

When she got home, Gracie was surprised to see Kevin Huling sitting on the steps of her front porch. Uncle Miltie had gone to Barry's Barber Shop earlier, and knowing his fondness for hanging out there, she didn't expect him back much before supper. He usually hitched a ride back with one of the regulars.

When Kevin merely looked up at her, she sat herself down beside him. "You've probably discovered by now that my uncle isn't home."

He nodded.

"I'm sure you can catch him at Barry's."

He still said nothing.

"Feel like some cookies and milk with me?"

He looked up, trying to gauge the sincerity of the offer.

"I've been running errands all day," she confessed. "I could use a snack, and eating alone is no fun. Sure you don't want to join me?"

A small grin played at the corners of his

lips. "Okay. Why not?"

"Well, don't just sit there. Come on!" Gracie said.

"I might be moving," he confided.

She was startled. "You just got here!"

"My dad has another job offer. It's a promotion, he says. But I've just started to make friends here."

"Have you talked to him about your feelings?"

"We had a big fight. That's how come I'm here. I ran away. I wanted to talk to Uncle Miltie, to have him pray with me."

Gracie felt her heart in her throat. *Help me now, Lord, as I know You will.*

"I can pray with you."

His eyes moistened, causing the boy to lower his gaze. "There's one more thing. My dad picked me up at school today. I knew something was up because he never comes home that early."

Kevin's face tightened. "He was all excited, like my feelings didn't matter at all. He just wanted to talk about *his* news, no matter how it affected the rest of us. He's always pushing me to get involved at school and play sports, to be a big jock like he was. But I can't make myself something I'm not. I'm short and skinny, and that's how it is. Why can't he accept that?"

Gracie listened, holding him in her heart in prayer.

"I'm not exactly their dream child. My mom expects a doctor or a rocket scientist."

He nibbled at his cookie, obviously struggling with tears.

"Uncle Miltie says you're very smart. You know a lot about history and lots of other things."

"But I don't get good grades. Uncle Miltie is the only person who sees me how I really am." He made a face.

"Maybe I'm really the reason my parents are talking divorce. Who'd want a jerk like me anyway?"

"Divorce? I thought you said you were moving!"

"My dad says he and my mom need some time to think things over. He says it's a separation, but that's what they always tell kids. My mom just cries."

Lord, this hurting family is in need of Your help. Wrap this poor boy in Your love, help him feel secure in the new friendships he's made in our church family.

He rubbed his eyes. "Nobody cares how I feel."

Just then, Uncle Miltie appeared at the back door. Gracie stood to greet her uncle, trying to catch his eye.

"Hey, did you hear about the two men from the monastery who opened a fast-food seafood restaurant?"

Before Gracie could alert her uncle, Kevin shot back with, "One was the *fish friar* and the other a *chip monk*."

"You're quick on the draw, kid."

Kevin smiled, and though it may have been forced, Gracie understood that seeing her uncle made him genuinely happy. "I saw that one on the Internet, too. You're going to have to dive deeper into cyberspace than Joke-A-Day."

"You want to practice our routine?" Uncle Miltie beamed, seemingly oblivious to the tears drying on Kevin's cheeks.

Maybe it's best this way, Lord. We are in Your hands.

Gracie excused herself and headed to her garden to pick tomatoes for their supper salad.

Marge was out in her own backyard with Charlotte. Gooseberry reclined on Marge's patio table, pointedly ignoring the Shih Tzu's barking at the delivery truck in the back alley.

Marge scooped up Charlotte, stroking and cooing to the small dog. "She hates un-invited guests. I tell her that we may be en-tertaining angels unaware. It doesn't matter

— she never trusts them."

Gracie walked over to scratch Gooseberry behind the ears. "Things are never as they seem. Maybe pets sense that."

"What's up?" Marge cut to the chase.

"Kevin Huling turned up on my doorstep this afternoon in need of TLC."

"How come?"

"He's having a tough time at home — thinks his family may be moving."

Gracie faced her friend. "Oh, Marge, I feel so helpless. There are so many hurting kids — parents, too — in Willow Bend. It's supposed to be different here."

"And it *is*." Marge sat down on the edge of the table. "He came to you. Where else could he sit on a doorstep and instantly get invited in, no questions asked. And for Kevin, Uncle Miltie is Santa and Superman rolled into one pun-loving grandpa figure."

"He's with him now."

"So, let God work."

Gracie scooped Gooseberry into her lap. "I thought I'd give them time — and space, just what you're suggesting."

"Follow me." Marge motioned toward her kitchen. "I've been invited to speak to the local businesswomen's association. They're going to ask you to cater, so I know

I'll have moral support."

Jeffrey Larson greeted them from the other room. "I found your file, Mrs. Lawrence. You just put it in the wrong place."

"Computers. Can't work with 'em, can't work without 'em." Marge walked over to talk to Jeffrey for a minute.

Gracie took the dishes from the drainer and started to put them away in the cupboard. She could hear Marge laughing. Jeffrey sounded respectful, which was a pleasant change.

"That kid is becoming indispensable. I'm going to have to put him on the payroll pretty soon," Marge said, rejoining her in the kitchen.

Gracie said, "You certainly seem to be a good influence on him."

"He didn't see much point in me in the beginning, when Pastor Paul matched us up. I kind of forced it when I asked for computer help. It wasn't long until I discovered that what Jeffrey really needed was an advocate. Kids can be awfully cruel, and he doesn't seem to realize how he turns people off. What he needs now is a good friend his own age, one who'll be supportive . . . and honest with him."

A thought came to Gracie. "Why not Kevin?"

Marge glanced toward the room where the boy was working. "Jeff has a hard time making friends."

"No harm trying." Gracie still liked the idea. "The two of them could load those boxes for Hazel. It would save Pastor Paul the trip."

"Great!"

"So you'll help me arrange it?"

"No problem."

They went on to discuss the menu for the upcoming birthday bash. Then Jeffrey appeared in the doorway.

"I heard you talking. Is there something you want me to do?"

Gracie smiled. "Just go and tell Uncle Miltie where I am, please. And if Kevin's still there, why don't you invite him to Youth Fellowship?"

"He's not cool." Jeffrey made a face.

Marge eyed him. "Trust me. Kevin could be a real friend if you let him. Okay?"

Gracie looked at Marge, surprised at her bluntness.

"Go invite the kid to Youth Fellowship," Marge told him. "Now."

As he headed out the door, Marge chuckled. Gracie was still staring at her.

"Wow, you certainly cut to the chase!"

"He thinks when I boss him around it's

funny. But his mom — a different story altogether."

It was clear that Jeffrey and Marge were forging a special relationship.

Gracie glanced at her watch. "Well, I suppose I better get back. Uncle Miltie will be complaining that he's famished."

"So, what's new?"

Gracie laughed. "Join us for supper?"

"Thought you'd never ask."

Rocky turned up in time for the soup course, so Marge set the table for four.

"Kevin needs a buddy his own age," Uncle Miltie agreed. "But we'll see if he and Jeffrey can get past each other's well-built defenses."

"Speaking of building, I hear there's a petition going around to develop proposals for that property at the edge of town. I'm sure Nick Kendrick is behind it, since several of the people sponsoring it are working for his campaign," Marge said.

"He's got to have money," Uncle Miltie reminded him.

"I hear that's all taken care of," she answered.

Gracie turned to face Rocky. "He hasn't somehow gotten access to the Rohleder estate, has he?"

Rocky shrugged. "I don't know. But rumors abound."

"Well, they better not count their chickens so soon," Marge warned. "Hazel's gearing up to act. Finally. She's going to make her sister's desire known. She's going to get a lawyer. How that's going to end up, I don't know, but I'm rooting for her."

"Who's representing her?" Rocky asked.

"Ann O'Neill." Marge looked triumphant. It had been her idea, after all.

Gracie cautioned, "We *think*. Nobody's talked to her yet."

Rocky took a deep breath. "Make sure she has all the information. Kendrick requested Hazel's driving record, Herb told me today. He's worried about being called as a witness."

"Is there anything we can do to help?" Marge wanted to know.

Rocky smiled. "You probably already are — keep praying. Nick Kendrick is one savvy lawyer."

12

It didn't take more than a telephone call to convince Hazel she needed to go see Ann O'Neill immediately. She had just received word that Nick Kendrick was in fact petitioning for a court-appointed administrator for Mabel's estate.

"I am not senile," Hazel declared. "What does he think he's up to?"

Gracie calmed her down and promised to come right over.

"By the way, Kathleen and I have had a row."

Gracie felt the chill across the phone line. "Is there anything I can do to help?"

"Get her another job."

She closed her eyes, praying for wisdom. "Will you both be there when I arrive?"

"I'll refrain from killing her until you get here."

Gracie called Ann and Pastor Paul, and prayed.

As she arrived at Hazel's door, Gracie gave herself a little pep talk. Just listen and don't make any hasty judgments, she reminded herself. Maybe the fuss has already died down.

Gracie followed Hazel into the parlor.

"Ann O'Neill and Pastor Paul are on the way," Gracie told her.

Hazel seemed satisfied and excused herself to gather the necessary paperwork.

"How did your test go?" Gracie asked Kathleen.

The young woman kept her focus on her task. "I'll have to make it up."

"Oh," was all Gracie could think to say.

Kathleen turned to face her. Her cheeks were flushed. "You might as well know . . . I skipped it. I didn't take the final. But what does it matter? It's not like I'm going to have a job, after all this."

"What?"

"I'm a traitor. Didn't Hazel tell you? I betrayed everyone. Everything bad you thought about me is true."

Gracie wanted to ask how this young woman knew what she had been thinking, but she held her tongue instead. *Lord, please lead me.*

"I said, I sold Hazel out!"

Gracie closed her eyes, sending up a quick prayer for spiritual first-aid assistance.

"That's why I broke up with my boyfriend

Nick. I told him it was treacherous. You don't live with someone, exploit their weakness and then move on. I couldn't go through with it."

Gracie met her gaze. "I'm confused, dear."

"Don't tell me that Hazel didn't tell you! She's livid. Nick Kendrick is calling me as a witness to her competency. I could have lied. But I told the truth. Sometimes she *does* scare me. She forgets important things. Not big things — little things, like turning off the stove or that she just watered a plant.

"The problem is, I didn't want to love her. But I do. Who wouldn't? But what does it matter now, anyway?"

"It matters to you. I can see that."

"Tell Hazel that. Oh, that Nick was so sweet — but all along he was taking advantage of me. I hate him now. And I hate myself!"

Gracie was still confused. "What happened?""

"He intercepted me at school. He wanted me to sign a document saying she isn't capable of taking care of herself. He used me."

"And Hazel found out."

"Of course she found out. He told her. She called him after she got that letter. You

171

had encouraged her to take charge, re-member?"

"Nick even told her that I might be willing to take money from her for my silence. He said that he was representing her best inter-ests. *Hah!* Nick Kendrick looks out for him-self."

Kathleen looked at Gracie, her lips quiv-ering. "I hate myself!"

"Do you have classes this afternoon?" Gracie asked.

Kathleen shook her head. She began to sob.

Gracie called Ann on her cell phone. She wanted her to know right away what had happened. Pastor Paul was already en route, so Gracie trusted God to guide the minister toward understanding the situa-tion.

Gracie fixed tea. She sat down, and closed her eyes, ready to listen to God.

Lord, we've troubles here, big troubles only You can resolve. I need You at this table this af-ternoon.

Hazel sipped tea from a mug, as Kathleen studied her from her post at the window. Neither woman had said anything to the other. Gracie glanced at her watch. Ann and Paul would be arriving any minute.

"Thank you, Gracie," Hazel told her. "Lying down helped, but I'm sorry that you've been put in the middle of this."

Paul's car pulled into the driveway, with Ann's right behind him. Kathleen went to get the door.

"Are you sure you want to do this?" Gracie looked at Hazel. "I feel that it's awkward for you both."

"I'm okay," Hazel replied. "I need to get on with this, no more excuses."

Paul's expression showed the sense of helplessness he felt. He sat quietly while Ann took notes as she asked Hazel questions.

"You really should have made sure she called me earlier," Ann said to Gracie. "However, that's water under the bridge. Let's see what we can figure out now. It doesn't sound like Kendrick has much of a case."

"This really is a beautiful house," Paul said to Hazel. Small talk wasn't easy, but he was trying. "Mabel said your father built it."

"In fact, my grandfather was the architect," Hazel said.

Ann smiled. "I've always admired it. We were all glad that you and Mabel moved back here. So many of these wonderful old

173

homes get turned into apartments or torn down."

"We decided early on to retire here. That was part of the agreement between our uncle and us. We promised we'd care for our aunt, and living here was part of the bargain. He wanted it to stay in the family. That way Mabel and I always knew that we'd have a home to return to."

"Your uncle provided for you both in his will very generously. And Kline and Paige have been well compensated for administering the estate. But I note that you've not drawn on that account in years."

"We never needed to," Hazel stated.

The lawyer scribbled something on her pad.

"My uncle and aunt married late in life. They never had children. My father was a good bit younger, the child of a second marriage. But he and his brothers were close."

Hazel took a sip of tea. "They adored us, really. They never had children of their own. By the time we came to live with Uncle Horace, he was almost fifty."

Kathleen looked up, her gaze resting on her employer.

"That must have been hard for you," Paul said.

"Not really. Mabel and I had the run of

the place. We would hide in the little closet under the bend in the staircase, where it climbed to the third floor, when we'd gotten ourselves into a pickle and were afraid to face the consequences."

Paul leaned forward, listening with attention.

"It was pitch dark in the closet, but cozy, too. There were shelves of warm bedding. Now, it's Lillian's favorite hiding spot."

Gracie glanced at Kathleen. The young woman was listening intently, too.

"We would huddle in our little hideaway, all tingly with fascination as we listened to the creaks and groans of the house." Hazel was savoring the memories. "We would shudder, imagining all kinds of delicious reasons why the old place was noisily rattling its bones."

Hazel leaned back in her chair, once again fully in the present. "Yes, Mabel and I have loved it here. My parents began their marriage here with my father's uncle and my grandmother. I cannot bear the thought of departing this world from any other place." She looked at Ann. "Can you do something to help me keep it?"

Ann touched her arm. "I'll do my best. I promise you that."

Paul told her about the recent letter he'd

received from Kendrick's office. Kathleen stirred her tea, her gaze downturned. Gracie lifted the young woman up in prayer.

"The situation is complicated by the fact that, before now, Hazel hasn't stepped forward to act on her part as administrator for Mabel," Ann told them. "Nick Kendrick has called that to the court's attention."

Ann looked at Hazel with a serious expression. "I hate to be repeating myself, but you should have handled this immediately. Kendrick's only doing his job."

Hazel's expression was unreadable.

Ann reviewed the notes she'd scribbled on the pad in front of her. "Kendrick will have to present evidence that he is the best person to administer the will."

Paul broke in. "But Hazel is the best choice for administrator! She's Mabel's closest living relative."

"There's no disputing that — unless her competency is called into question, which it has now been," Ann informed him.

Kathleen sank down in her chair, her face lowered.

Ann seemed uncomfortable with saying more. She looked at Kathleen and then back to Hazel. "We may have a fight on our hands."

"Kathleen has made herself a part of

this," Hazel said calmly. "If she's going to betray me, so be it, but I'd like her to be part of the discussion. She needs to understand the consequences of her actions."

"I didn't mean it!" Kathleen protested. "I was wrong!"

"If I am incapable of managing my own affairs, then I want to hear a case for it." Hazel stared at Kathleen.

Kathleen repeated, "I was wrong, okay? I told Nick you often confused me for your sister. It seemed harmless at the time."

Gracie wanted to be sympathetic.

Hazel sat serenely regarding the young woman she'd invited into her home and into her confidence. Gracie could see that Paul, to his Christian credit, made Kathleen feel better when he told her, "We all do stupid things."

"It didn't feel stupid. We were just talking, Nick and I, making conversation about my job and my experiences with the elderly. He was asking questions. I wanted to impress him. How was I to know how he was going to use what I said against Hazel?"

"Do you think that I'm senile, Kathleen?" Hazel claimed her employee's attention. "Well, do you? Please!"

Kathleen kept her head down.

"Look at me and answer!" Hazel commanded her. "Tell me, Kathleen, what has been your experience these last months?"

Kathleen started crying.

It was Gracie's turn to soothe, as she reached over to touch Hazel's shoulder. "She's suffering and I'm sure she's sorry. Isn't that right, dear?"

"I didn't say I was sorry!" Kathleen wailed. "She didn't give me a chance! I confessed, and then she jumped all over me, accusing me of being out to get her money." She rubbed her eyes, trying to stop the tears from welling up. "It has nothing to do with money."

"We have a problem to solve," Ann told them, "a problem that needs clear thinking and resolve. Kathleen, I sense you want to do what is best for Hazel. You seem like a level-headed, caring young woman."

Kathleen relaxed slightly, hearing these words.

Ann turned to Hazel. "And, Hazel, they are right, you *are* the natural choice to take charge of Mabel's estate. Of course, you should have filed before now, but the court should honor your claim."

"So, there'll be no problem?" Paul was hopeful.

Ann turned back to Hazel. "I'm going to

be blunt. Kendrick does have a case. You've not responded to the court order to settle the estate. You have four traffic citations in a little over a year. The chief of police has taken you home on several occasions when you became disoriented. Nick Kendrick knows all of this."

Hazel's lower lip trembled, but she held Ann's gaze.

Ann continued. "Thankfully, you have no moving violations. But Hazel, we've still got a problem. We've got to prove to a court that you're still in control of your mental faculties. We need Kathleen, if she is willing, to testify that she was coerced. Now, if you two can get beyond your differences, we will plan your defense."

"Why do I have to defend myself?" Hazel wanted to know. "It ought be his responsibility to prove me incompetent."

Ann's smile was wry. "Because he thinks you won't fight back. And you haven't, up until now. Don't play into his hands, Hazel. We all have to work together."

Hazel was listening intently. But, then, so was everyone.

"Listen to me," Ann said. "The important thing is to get our strategy and stick to it. You're an acclaimed artist, Hazel, entitled to some eccentricities. The court will allow you leeway. You've got good friends in this room who believe in you. Let's put the hard feelings behind us — what do you say?"

Hazel looked at Kathleen. "All right."

"I like you." Kathleen held her gaze. "I wish things had gone differently. I'm not going to testify against you, Hazel. I promise."

"Hazel will have many witnesses attesting to the wonderful care she provided for her sister," Paul said.

"I'm going to note all of that in a letter to the judge," Ann told them. "I am going to enclose a letter from Kathleen, and then, be sure I will confront Mr. Kendrick with our knowledge of his impropriety. I'm certain he'll privately want to avoid any embarrassment, since this is an election year."

Ann paused. "Frankly, I don't believe Nick Kendrick wants to make a case out of this. He's hoping Hazel will do nothing, just as she has up until now. That makes it easy for him.

"That doesn't let you off the hook, Hazel. From now on, you need to pay attention to details — the first being securing a will of your own."

"I'll make an appointment," Hazel promised her.

"It's made. Tomorrow at ten. Gracie, or maybe even Kathleen, can bring you by."

Gracie nodded, thankful for Ann's calm efficiency.

"I can attest to Mabel's understanding that Hazel would be her administrator," Paul told Ann. "Do you need me to sign anything?"

"I hope that's not necessary, for Hazel's sake as well as your own."

Ann glanced over her notes again. "Hazel can speak for her sister. The estate will be settled according to her wishes, but the first thing to establish is that Hazel is the rightful and capable administrator. If you could find that will, Hazel, that would be the biggest help."

Gracie updated her on their progress. "We're at an impasse."

"Has anyone considered that she might have used a tape recorder? Clients bring cassettes to me all the time."

Hazel was sure Mabel hadn't owned one.

"Those little pocket models are popular. Mabel knew she was dying. A tape recorder would be the easiest way to transcribe her intentions."

"I've seen nothing resembling anything like that, is all I can say," Hazel told her.

Gracie looked at Kathleen, whose expression remained inscrutable.

Ann went over the outline of the letter she planned to draft on Hazel's behalf.

"I hear the *Gazette*'s sponsoring an art exhibit," Paul said, looking to strike a lighter note.

Ann looked up. "An art exhibit?"

"Featuring local artists," Gracie explained.

"I guess I'm to be the first," Hazel added.

"I didn't realize you were working again," Ann said.

"Actually, there's been a gallery in Chicago wanting to show my sculptures."

Ann's face broke into a wide grin. "Why didn't you tell me this before? Hazel, what am I going to do with you? You don't need a guardian as much as a manager." The lawyer paused. "I'm going to call Mr. Kendrick and ask him whether or not he supports the arts. Do you have the letter from the gallery? It might just be the way to get this whole thing dropped."

Gracie looked at her, perplexed.

"The court doesn't want to waste its time on a case like this. Nick Kendrick doesn't, either. He can't win — and, again, it's an election year."

"Will Hazel be able to honor her sister's bequest?" Gracie wondered.

Ann looked at Gracie over the top of her glasses. "At this point, we still don't know what Mabel wanted. Nonetheless, we can certainly push for Hazel to be able to make the decision. The point is, she's a working sculptor with a professional reputation. Everyone knows artists in the throes of creativity can be absentminded!"

Hazel grinned at her. "If you put it like that, even I might believe you," she joked.

When Jessica Larson turned up at the planning meeting for the Rohleder celebration party, things started to heat up. Eternal Hope's president of the board had a reputation for confrontation, and she arrived with her gloves on.

Don Delano offered her a chair. "We haven't gotten started yet."

Jessica sat down, but said nothing.

"Okay, let's see if we have this right. Hazel Rohleder is covering all the expenses for this party, right?" Bert Benton scanned the report. "And, Gracie, you agreed to cater."

It would be a simple fare, soup and fixings. "Of course we'll have a cake and ice cream," she told him. "Marge sent out the invitations, and I think we can expect about a hundred people. It's also the night before the opening of Hazel's art show at the *Gazette* building, so there will likely be a few out-of-town friends."

Bert added, "And I have a note here that the Fellowship Committee is going to serve and clean up. Looks like everything's covered."

Jessica toyed with the large diamond ring on her right hand.

"We have a musical tribute planned," Barb Jennings reminded him. "We've included favorite songs from the thirties on, and we'll feature a lovely Fanny Crosby hymn medley. The Hardings are going to perform as a family. Rick wrote and arranged the piece. Isn't that something to look forward to?"

Bert put a check next to the entertainment item on his meeting agenda.

"Are we going to recognize Hazel in any special way?" Marge wanted to know.

"I think the best gift we can give her is to honor her twin," Barb said. "The party will take something from all of us and make it into the sort of harmony that Mabel always encouraged."

Gracie looked at Barb. "Maybe you could say a few words about that. You were close to the sisters, and I think sharing some of your memories of them would help the community realize how special they are to all of us."

"I do have some old photographs," Barb told them. "I was thinking of making a book."

"I could help you," Marybeth offered. "I love doing that sort of thing."

Don Delano raised his hand. "I'll take some snapshots that evening and get them to you, Marybeth, to complete the album."

"The church has already received a few gifts in Mabel's honor," Pastor Paul told them. "So, if anyone wishes to donate, we'll make sure it's acknowledged that night, too."

"Has anyone considered the awkward position we are in?" Jessica suddenly broke in. "Our pastor has put us in a compromising position — in direct contradiction to the best interest of this community, in fact."

Paul was clearly embarrassed, but when Gracie opened her mouth to say something that might ease the situation, Jessica cut her off.

"The Rohleder estate is important to Willow Bend. We have been using the interest for years to offer college scholarships to worthy high school seniors, and now we have the opportunity to utilize the principal.

"We can make an investment in the future

of Willow Bend in an even more practical way than the scholarships are doing. And, we can earn a tidy profit to boot."

Bert took off his glasses. "Jessica, you're not offering anything that makes any sense. What do you mean?"

"The Rohleder principal should be invested in Willow Bend property. We can make change happen. Let's look to the future and not the past!"

"How handy, for a woman who sells real estate!" Marge said pointedly.

"When they put in the new highway, that piece of land at the edge of town will be even more valuable. This church is standing in the way." Jessica pursed her lips as she said this.

"What does Eternal Hope have to do with that?" Bert wanted to know. "Besides, we're your church, too."

"Hazel Rohleder can make that happen. There's enough in the estate to keep her comfortable until the day she dies. But Paul is encouraging her in an inappropriate way to divert Mabel's portion."

Paul stood. "I've done nothing of the sort! Mabel Rohleder *wanted* to leave her money to Eternal Hope. I was just there to listen. And I only wanted to honor her request. Now, I see that I cannot stay for this conversation."

"This is neither the time nor the place, Jessica," Bert warned sternly.

But Jessica continued, undaunted. "Neither Hazel nor Mabel are heirs to the Rohleder estate. The rightful heir is Willow Bend and the future. It galls me to see Horace's dream thwarted by sentimentality. Mabel is gone, and Hazel is barely able to look after herself. What right does Eternal Hope have to get involved? Let the lawyers determine if she is competent."

Marge was indignant. "When did you get a vested interest in this case, Jessica? What makes *you* so sure what Horace Rohleder intended?"

"As I understand it, the bequest to Eternal Hope does not involve the Rohleder estate," Bert Benton told them. "Mabel had assets and wanted those to go to our church. I think we are confusing the two."

Gracie faced Jessica. "The purpose of this committee is to coordinate fellowship events, and right now we are planning a birthday party to honor one of our own."

Jessica merely looked bored.

"I think Bert made it clear. Mabel's estate is separate. And, furthermore, as you well know, Pastor Paul is a loyal, dedicated and godly man, a blessing for us all."

"Think what you're saying, Jessica! This

whole discussion will only be an embarrassment after the will turns up," Marge warned
her.

"*If* there is a will." Jessica was determined
to have the last word.

Bert took the floor. "The meeting is over.
Sorry, Jessica." He then asked Gracie to
lead them in a closing prayer.

13

Kevin arrived at Gracie's after school to help move the boxes from Hazel's house. Marge was closing her shop and then picking up Jeffrey, so Gracie had time to get to know Kevin a little better. And whether boys or men, the best way to the male heart was via the stomach. She sliced a piece of freshly baked gingerbread.

"Do you like whipped cream?"

His grin cinched it, so she lathered the square. "You get the first piece. Uncle Miltie loves it, but he had a pressing appointment for a checkers match this afternoon. You know, he's in that county competition at the senior center."

"He'll win hands down." Kevin took a big gulp of milk. "He's a shrewd player, all right, the only problem is his face is a dead giveaway. I was giving him pointers. It's all in the body language and expressions. I learned that in drama class. And, I'm happy to say, Uncle Miltie now has deadpan down pat."

Gracie didn't want to spoil anything by telling him he always had.

"And even if he can't beat them at checkers, he's sure to kill them with his jokes."

Gracie laughed. "I can tell you two have been spending too much time together."

"My dad moved out," Kevin now said. "Mom says we're not going. She loves her job at Kline and Paige. Dad says he needs time, but he didn't take the new job. Mom says they're going to work it out, since twenty years of marriage is too valuable just to toss away."

He looked at Gracie. "I hope she's right."

"She is, but let's pray your dad realizes it. God can mend a broken marriage. His stitches will create something stronger and more beautiful."

Gracie took his hand and asked God to guide Kevin's parents. "Wrap them securely in Your love, help them to grow through this and draw closer to You. Amen."

She told him, "There's nothing we can't handle with God beside us. Remember that, Kevin."

"God is really easier to talk to than most people."

She smiled. "Yes, He is. I'm glad you've discovered that."

"My mom prays, but it was Uncle Miltie who made me realize how easy it is to talk to God. He prayed with me, too. He said that prayer was not a way to get what I want, but a way to become what God wants me to be."

Gracie liked that, and was proud of her uncle. "That's exactly the right way to look at it."

"I really want to stay in Willow Bend."

"I know you do."

Kevin took another bite of gingerbread. "This is the perfect job for my mom — her first full-time one. She does research, which she's great at. Dad says she could find the undotted *i* in an encyclopedia. She's had experience doing courthouse research for lawyers, searching titles, stuff like that.

"When I was little, we used to take picnics to the cemetery." He grinned. "That's where I thought everyone went for a picnic. Mom did genealogy stuff for other people, too."

"She sounds like an interesting woman." Gracie made a mental note to really talk to Kevin's mother one day soon, get to know her better.

"You'd like her. I know she likes you already." He furrowed his brow. "She's going to talk to you and Uncle Miltie about me going on that youth retreat. It's to some church camp in the woods." He made a face.

"And you don't want to go?"

He shook his head and pulled in his shoulders, concentrating on what was left of the gingerbread.

"Do you know Jeffrey Larson?"

Kevin didn't look up. "Sure."

"I just wondered."

"The other kids don't like him." His tone was matter-of-fact.

"Uncle Miltie says you're the fastest guy with a punchline he's met in a long time." Gracie shifted gears.

"But he's an old man, and it's not too cool to hang out with an old dude either, for that matter."

Friends were just what the boy needed. "I like Jeffrey. He's just a little different, that's all," she told him.

Kevin only shrugged.

"We're all a little afraid of being rejected. Making friends seems scary, so we silently hope the other person will make the first move. Somebody has to take the risk, Kevin."

Kevin stared at her. "Let somebody else."

"You could be missing a great opportunity."

"Now you sound like my mom."

Gracie smiled. "It's an occupational hazard."

"Good one, Mrs. Parks." Kevin shoveled the last big bite of gingerbread into his mouth. "I guess it can't hurt getting to know Jeff better."

"This place is awesome," Kevin told Hazel as they joined her in the studio to retrieve the last of the boxes.

"My dad thinks I should concentrate on math and science," he went on. "But I like art. Always did."

Jeffrey pushed his glasses back up on his nose. "My mom says I should be a doctor. I get good grades and they make lots of money."

"What do *you* want to be?" Hazel asked Jeffrey.

"A pilot." Jeffrey had second thoughts. "I don't know, I guess it's a dumb dream.

"I like to draw cartoons, and kids say I'm pretty funny. Uncle Miltie says I'm good at history, too. He says I'd make a good political cartoonist. But I don't know what I want to do."

Hazel picked up the chisel. "My uncle thought I should be a nurse or a teacher."

"But you decided to be an artist anyway," Kevin said.

"My aunt talked my uncle into allowing me to study art, but she was secretly hoping that I'd change my mind. She thought I should become a teacher, too."

Hazel looked past them, remembering. "She told my sister years later at the opening of one of my New York shows, that she couldn't be prouder, and that she'd finally given up her hope that I would move home to Willow Bend to teach."

"You followed your dream," Kevin said, softly.

Hazel put her hand on his shoulder. "Yes, I did."

She made eye contact with both boys. "Follow your dreams, but stay grounded in family and community. You need them more than you know at this point in your life."

"We're always moving," Kevin said. "So why bother making friends when you just have to leave?"

Jeffrey surprised them with, "You move away. So what? You can be friends for a day."

"That friend could end up a best friend," Gracie reminded him.

"Nobody likes me," Kevin insisted. "I know it."

Jeffrey shrugged. "So, that makes two of us."

"Yeah," Kevin decided.

"Well you two can start carrying these boxes out to the car." Marge winked. "We can talk more about friendships when the heavy lifting's finished!"

Kevin handed Jeffrey a large box.

"Hey!" Jeffrey balked at the weight.

"What are friends for?" Kevin flashed a swift grin.

Gracie and Marge followed Hazel to the dining room where she wanted to show them something. "I'd about given up on finding the will, and then I discovered this note. It was just a scrap, but look what it says."

" 'Don't forget the way home.' " Gracie looked at Hazel, perplexed. "What does that mean?"

"Uncle Horace used to tell us that when we went off somewhere, whether it was to youth camp, college or to make our own way in the world. He'd always hug us hard, and say, 'Don't forget the way home.' "

"Why do you suppose Mabel wrote that?" Marge asked the question before Gracie could.

Hazel studied her sister's handwriting, as if it would give up its secret with greater concentration. "Those last weeks, Mabel spent most of her conscious hours reliving the past. Even if I don't know what it means, I don't want to throw it away. I sense it's important. Mabel was trying to tell me something."

Hazel put the note down, but not without first casting a regretful glance at it.

"Or, was she trying to tell me something else? Uncle Horace was methodical. And so was Mabel. She wrote a will, Gracie, I'm sure of it."

Marge now picked up the card. "Could *home* mean something else? Something that only you would understand?"

"I've searched my mind. There's something here, I sense it, but. . . ."

"And no more clues?" Gracie asked.

"Kathleen and I sorted everything last night."

Gracie was glad Hazel had forgiven her young friend.

"Where's Kathleen?" Marge asked.

"In Avery with her friends. We both thought it wise to put a bit of time and distance between us. She lived with them before coming here. It will help us mend further."

Curious still about Kathleen's own history, Gracie asked Hazel what she knew of it. She could provide little information about Kathleen other than that she was an only child, and that her mother had died a year earlier.

"She told me that last evening, as we worked," Hazel went on. "Kathleen so wanted to please me, I knew — she was trying to make it up to me in her own way. I understood."

The rest that Hazel told them was that Kathleen had been raised by a single mother. "Her mother was bitter that she'd grown up without a father. But then she did the same to Kathleen, divorcing her husband when Kathleen was little."

"Oh, dear," Gracie said.

"Her mother died years ago, and after that Kathleen got closer to her father. He was paralyzed as a result of an auto accident, and he drank. She moved to Mason City to take care of him. He died a few months before she came to work for us."

"How did she get involved with Nick Kendrick?" Gracie wanted to know.

"He teaches a class at the community college she attends. It's about the legal responsibilities of home-care providers. He sought her out, and they ended up going out to dinner."

Hazel fingered the ribbon holding a pack of old letters. "These were from Uncle

Horace while we were living in New York. I didn't know Mabel had saved them." She sighed.

Marge sympathized, "Your uncle would never have wished this trouble on you."

Hazel sighed again. "Ann's got her work cut out for her. I'll be honest, I do lose my bearings sometimes. Maybe Nick Kendrick isn't so far off. I relied on Mabel far too much, and now she's gone."

"But you had to handle everything in the end," Marge reminded her. "You did it, Hazel, so give yourself credit."

"I barely got by, as that stack of late notices attests," Hazel countered. "I've ignored the correspondence from the lawyers, government and bank. Everyone's right to be irritated at my laxness — sometimes emotions swamp your common sense. It's hard to be practical when all you can feel is your loss."

Barb Jennings was already at the organ when Gracie arrived at church early for choir practice. She'd hoped to catch Pastor Paul before he left for the day, but the office was dark. She headed for the choir loft ahead of the others.

"I'm glad to have a chance to talk to you alone," Barb said as she finished the piece.

They hugged. Then Barb said, "Gracie, this party we're planning — it's going to be so lovely!"

"They meant a lot to you, I know," Gracie told her.

"Hazel and Mabel have lived here for the last few years unnoticed. They came back quietly, moved to their family's home and just blended right in. They didn't ask anything of anyone."

Gracie herself had not reached out to the women. Yet, it hadn't been deliberate. The Rohleder sisters had kept to themselves, and it had been easy to let it go at that. She said, "We should have made more of an effort to include them in community life."

"They've been so independent that we took it for granted that they wanted it that way. I'm worried about Hazel, Gracie. Can she do it on her own? Right now, our church family is all she has."

Gracie had no response, but sat down in the seat closest to the organ. Hazel obviously had a streak of steel in her, but age had a way of undermining will.

"People are saying that it's in Hazel's best interest to let a second party control her life. She shouldn't be living alone, and the estate provides generously to have her taken care of. That would solve everything so neatly.

But I don't like it, Gracie."

Gracie tried to think. She knew God was working on Hazel's behalf.

"Oh, Gracie, what are we to do?" Barb broke in on her thoughts.

"Trust Him," came as naturally as her breath. "Let's just honor Hazel with this party. The Lord will handle the rest."

When Gracie returned from choir practice, Uncle Miltie and Rocky were putting the finishing touches on the shelves they'd installed in the new garden shed.

"It's gorgeous!" she told them.

They both beamed proudly.

Gracie now asked, "Ready for a snack? How about some jam tarts?"

"*Wow!*" they chorused in unison.

As they sat down in the kitchen, Gracie told them what she'd learned about Kathleen Bailey's background.

"I don't know why," Rocky speculated, "but I have a hunch there's more to this than meets the eye. There's something about Kathleen Bailey, and I think Gracie's on the right track."

"Sleuth sense," Uncle Miltie decided. "That's why she's so good at solving mysteries. She's also read just about every one on the library shelves!"

Rocky pointed out, "You know, Horace Rohleder was worth more than a few million. He took a few risks on the technology stocks of the day and was in on the ground floor when profits began rolling in. What's more, the firm Kendrick works for has done an excellent job in managing the estate."

"What does that mean to Hazel and Eternal Hope?" Uncle Miltie asked.

Rocky raised an eyebrow. "It means money, that's all. Bucks. Big ones. You have to remember that the people managing estates of this value have a stake in how they are disbursed. They make a profit, as well."

"It seems then that it's in their best interest to keep the money right where it is," Uncle Miltie said.

"Kendrick wants this money released to help his career. But you're right, Kline and Paige may have other ideas," Rocky said.

Gracie wondered. "Do they know what's going on?"

"Maybe Hazel ought to update them." Rocky waggled a finger. "There's more than one way to keep this story from ending badly for the good guys."

14

Gracie opened her door to face Kathleen Bailey. Her eyes were red and swollen. "Please help me."

Gracie put her arm around the girl and ushered her into the house. "You wash your face, and I'll put on the kettle."

Gracie did not know what to say, but Uncle Miltie greeted her with a wide smile. "You're in luck. I know where to find a few stray jam tarts."

But Kathleen told him she wasn't hungry, and he tactfully excused himself to go watch one of his favorite programs.

Gracie pretended to be shocked. "I think Uncle Miltie keeps a secret stash of jam tarts, holding a few in reserve every time I make them!"

Kathleen sat down and scooped Gooseberry into her lap. Gooseberry purred contentedly.

"Now, what's wrong?" Gracie took the seat across from her. "We were with Hazel yesterday and thought you'd patched things up. She said only kind things about you."

Kathleen stroked the large orange cat but didn't answer.

"She told us how you'd lost both your parents and your grandmother. You've had a lot of hurt in your young life."

"I've done a lot of stupid things."

Gracie patted her hand. "We all have, dear. God's forgiven you, so who are we to judge? Hazel doesn't hold a grudge."

"If you knew half of what I've done! I was pretty wild in high school, rebelling against my mother. She hated her mother. My grandmother was tough. She could push your buttons, all right. But she was an old lady. Mom wouldn't have anything to do with her, even when Grandma moved in with us after my mother's stroke."

Kathleen curled her lip. "My grandmother nursed my mother until she died of heart failure. But I actually never believed my mother had a heart to fail.

"Mom treated her mother horribly. I guess I was trying to pay her back for that — like Grandma needed my grief on top of everything else. When Mom died, I was really ashamed — guilty, really. I took off with my boyfriend."

She looked at Gracie, expecting her to be shocked.

"I bummed around until I got a letter telling me that Grandma had cancer. I went home to take care of her. It was the least I could do for all the pain I'd caused her. Like I said, she was a tough one, not given to accepting help.

"Funny, that's when I decided to go into health care. I didn't mind her being so grumpy — even nasty. After all, she was hurting. I could see it in her eyes.

"But it wasn't cancer that was so painful . . . it was something deeper. She wouldn't tell me, but I knew she was sorry about her relationship with my mother."

Gracie sighed, thinking how easily one bitter relationship soured another. Kathleen acted out the animosity her mother and grandmother could not seem to resolve. Pride and resentment seemed the natural way of things, and blessed reconciliation the unnatural.

"Maybe God was teaching you compassion. I think perhaps He was using you to help mend that broken relationship. You gave the love that your mother wasn't capable, at the time, of giving. Broken hearts can be mended more beautifully when the stitches are kindness and love."

Hadn't she just said much the same thing to Kevin? These poor children! *Lord, how it must pain You to see them struggle so.*

Kathleen shook her head. "You don't know the whole story. See, my grandmother did finally tell me the truth. She had destroyed all the letters my mother's father sent.

"But, when she died, I plotted to get back at the only people left to hurt — and I didn't even know them! Isn't that crazy? I wanted to hurt my grandfather's family. Then, wouldn't you know, my *dad* took sick. I stayed with him and his wife until he died last spring. That's how I ended up in Indiana."

Gracie did not know how to respond to these revelations. Where were they leading?

"Nick thought he was in control, that he was using me," Kathleen's tone was defiant. "Well, I duped him. I hold the trump card."

"Trump card?"

Kathleen turned defensive. "Let's just say I have one up on Mr. Nick Kendrick, and he knows it. He came to see me in Avery, all contrition and sweetness. I let him have it with both barrels!"

She stuck her chin out. "It's too late. I told him."

"What is, dear? *What* is it that you have on Mr. Kendrick?"

Kathleen shook her head. "This secret is

205

better left buried, I know that now. Actually, my dad told me. He didn't want me to approach a family that never knew I existed." She paused.

"I told Mabel almost everything. And you know what?" Kathleen was crying. "She reacted the same way you did. She said that God was merciful. That He did not look on the outside, but looked at the heart. Mabel said that it would all come out all right and to trust God on that.

"She said, too, that I was already forgiven. That's why I was so mad at you about the religion thing. I wanted to hate you all. I came here to take advantage of the Rohleders.

"I caused this problem," her voice was hoarse, "and now I'm fixing it! Hazel doesn't need me, she never has. She was wonderful with Mabel. It's time for me to just disappear. I just came from Hazel's. I went to get my stuff."

Gracie handed the girl a tissue.

"I said nasty things to Hazel. I pushed until she told me to get out. And then I didn't know where I was going. I came here expecting the same of you. I was sure that Hazel had already called you and that you would turn me away, too."

Gracie's chest tightened. *Oh, Lord, how*

can I help this frightened and confused young woman? "If you need a place until you figure things out, I've got another bedroom."

"No, I can't stay." She smiled sadly. "It's the end of the semester, and I've decided to transfer. But I really like working with older people. That's one good thing to come out of all this; I know now what I want to do with my life. And Grandma's money will provide that."

15

Lillian, dressed in red taffeta, braids bouncing with matching beads and ribbons, bounded into the Eternal Hope Family Living Center. Comfort followed, and then Rick entered with the guest of honor on his arm.

Hazel practically glided into the room in a soft black knit dress, over which she wore a red satin jacket with Chinese embroidery. She looked elegant, a visitor from a Paris salon or a New York City gallery.

It was too bad that Kathleen could not be here, Gracie thought sadly. She'd tried to convince her, but Kathleen had been adamant that the break was best. She was staying in Avery until Ann assured her that Nick was dropping the petition and that Hazel was being appointed administrator of her sister's estate.

Gracie suspected it had more to do with shame.

"Where do you want these?" Abe Wasserman stood in front of her with two large trays of homemade rolls.

As she directed Abe, Rocky appeared beside her to sample the relish tray.

"Nick Kendrick has resigned. I got word today that he's going to take a position in Indianapolis — closer to the action, I suppose."

"Well, that should lessen the push to develop that land, making use of the Rohleder estate."

He popped a cherry tomato into his mouth. "What's on the menu for tonight?"

"Chicken noodle soup, of course!" Abe exclaimed.

"Mother Wasserman's recipe," Gracie reminded him. "Abe was here this morning to make sure we used just the right sized pinch of mint. I also made my chili."

"Well, I can never get enough of either one," Rocky told them, and his stomach seconded the motion with a rumble.

Hazel cried over the elaborately decorated cake and through all the choruses of *Happy Birthday*. The Hardings' number was the highlight of the evening. It seemed a perfect finale to a perfect occasion.

Kevin and Jeffrey appeared with a large flat rectangle, wrapped in a linen sheet and decorated with a huge red bow. Pastor Paul joined them on the stage area.

"As you all know, there are *two* birthday girls." He put his arm around Hazel. "One of them couldn't be here with us tonight. She's in heaven, but I'm sure she's looking down on us and enjoying every moment."

Hazel smiled, her eyes bright with tears.

"Yesterday, Hazel called me. Mabel had wanted to give Eternal Hope a gift in appreciation for all the love and friendship she's received through the years. And that gift may yet be in the future. We'll see, but for now Hazel wanted us to have a different gift as a way of thanking us for our support."

Hazel now began to speak, slowly but confidently, with all the love she had in her, addressing the people gathered to honor her and her sister. Her eyes danced.

"Mabel found family here after the last of ours passed on. She played the organ for this church for a few years, and even when we lived hundreds of miles away she remained an active member, contributing financially to all the good you do."

She motioned for Kevin and Jeffrey to unveil her gift.

"I only ever did one painting. It was a gift to my uncle and a promise that we would never forget where we came from. It hung over the mantle in his study for a very long

210

time, until we moved it to my sister's room downstairs."

Kevin pulled the sheet off to reveal a lovely autumn landscape. It was a street in Willow Bend, with the Rohleder house at the far end and two women on a rain-slicked sidewalk.

The boys put it on the easel that stood there. "It's no masterpiece," Hazel explained. "But it's . . . home. It seems to belong to this room where you all come together in fellowship." She waved a farewell to the group and stepped aside. The little ceremony was ended.

Rick now joined Gracie. "You look happy," he told her.

"She is truly a remarkable woman. This occasion honoring her — and Mabel — is indeed a happy one."

"She was so excited to give the picture to the church. She only told Paul because she needed help in pulling it off. Paul shanghaied the boys. I stumbled on to the secret when I picked her up tonight. They were taking it to the car."

"And she actually now has a will, imagine that," Rick said. That makes *me* happy."

"Me, too," Gracie concurred.

Gracie concentrated on the painting again. It was an overcast day, the sky was

211

sluggishly gray, but the rose hues suggested sunrise. "Perhaps the sun is just about to come out," she said aloud, without realizing it.

"You're right," the artist, overhearing her, confirmed. "We're going home."

Then it hit Gracie. "That's the name of the painting, isn't it?"

"*The Way Home,*" Hazel said softly. Her eyes widened, and she smiled. Gracie did, too.

Rick looked uncertainly at them. "What is it?"

"Take the back off the painting!" Hazel commanded.

Gracie was polishing the last pedestal, as Hazel unpacked the final sculpture for display. What had begun as an impulse to stimulate a grieving woman had become a much anticipated event.

Gracie stood to survey Marge's accomplishment on the eve of the show's opening. It was hard to believe that until recently it had been an overlooked storage area, filled with rusty metal filing cabinets and cases of bottled water.

"Thank you for giving up this space," Hazel told him. "And your profile of me was beautifully done. I think you only misquoted me once — which is pretty good."

Rocky looked worried.

"I'm just teasing," Hazel reassured him.

Gracie was proud of all of their friends: the guys who'd given up evenings to serve on the paint crew; Roy Bell, who'd supervised the building of the cabinets and display cases; and the boys and girls who'd done the prep work, scrubbing walls and windows.

Little Lillian Harding suddenly came up to throw herself at Hazel. "Hello, darling girl," the elderly woman greeted her.

"Hi." Lillian turned shy.

Holding Lillian's hand, Hazel turned back to Gracie and Rocky. "Finding Mabel's will freed us all from the weight of suspicion that was poisoning the air. Eternal Hope has its bequest, and I have a new relation." She pointed at Kathleen, who was walking in the door just then.

"Hello, Cousin Hazel," Kathleen said, embracing her.

"Me, too!" squealed Lillian.

Rocky and Gracie smiled at each other over her head. Another mystery had been brought to a heartwarming conclusion.

RECIPE

Gracie's Spaghetti Pie

8 ounces thin spaghetti
2 eggs
¼ cup grated Parmesan cheese
½ cup chopped green pepper
½ cup chopped onion
2 tablespoons butter or margarine
1 cup sour cream
1 pound Italian-style sausage, casings removed
1 cup water
One 6 ounce can tomato paste
4 ounces shredded mozzarella

Break the spaghetti in half and cook it according to package instructions until it's al dente. Drain it. Beat together the eggs and the Parmesan cheese. Add this to the spaghetti and mix together well. Grease a ten-inch pie pan and line it with the spaghetti mixture. Set it aside.

Sauté the green pepper and onion in butter until the onion is just soft. Stir in the sour cream and then spoon this mixture into the spaghetti "crust." Cook the sausage in a heavy saucepan until it's no longer pink, breaking it up as it browns. Carefully drain off the fat, then add the water and tomato paste. Heat this until boiling, then reduce it and let it simmer uncovered for ten minutes. When this sauce is slightly thickened, stir it and then spoon over the sour cream mixture.

Cover the pie with foil and bake it in a preheated 350-degree oven for twenty-five minutes. Remove the foil and sprinkle the pie with grated mozzarella. Bake another five minutes or until the cheese is thoroughly melted.

Gracie says, "This rich and deliciously filling dish cuts most easily if you allow it to set for at least five minutes first. It also freezes perfectly."

About the Author

"I, like Gracie, love homemaking and cooking," writes **ROBERTA UPDEGRAFF**. "I married my high-school sweetheart, have been married for more than twenty-five years and have three-plus wonderful children. I say *plus* because our home seems to sprout teenagers and young adults, making our dinner table banter quite lively.

"I am a substitute teacher at Williamsport High School in Pennsylvania, and I love my students! I have taught everything from auto mechanics to orchestra. I am also a Sunday school teacher and volunteer youth leader.

"We continue our family's tradition by serving God as volunteers in mission. This summer we will return to Honduras for the fifth time to help with the ongoing reconstruction after Hurricane Mitch.

"I am a member of the St. David's Christian Writers' Conference board of directors, and I am active in West Branch Christian Writers. This is my seventh book in the 'Church Choir Mysteries' series."

A Note from the Editors

This original Guideposts Book was created by the Books and Inspirational Media Division of the company that publishes *Guideposts*, a monthly magazine filled with true stories of hope and inspiration.

Guideposts is available by subscription. All you have to do is write to Guideposts, 39 Seminary Hill Road, Carmel, New York 10512. When you subscribe, each month you can count on receiving exciting new evidence of God's presence, His guidance and His limitless love for all of us.

Guideposts Books are available on the World Wide Web at www.guidepostsbooks. com. Follow our popular book of devotionals, *Daily Guideposts*, and read excerpts from some of our best-selling books. You can also send prayer requests to our Monday morning Prayer Fellowship and read stories from recent issues of our magazines, *Guideposts*, *Angels on Earth*, and *Guideposts for Teens*.